THE
BOY
WHO
COULD
MAKE
HIMSELF
DISAPPEAR

By KIN PLATT

D0033764

Published by
Dell Publishing Co., Inc.
1 Dag Hammarskjold Plaza
New York, N.Y. 10017
Copyright © 1968 by Kin Platt
All Rights Reserved. For information, address
Chilton Book Company, Philadelphia, Pennsylvania.
Laurel-Leaf Library ® TM 766734, Dell Publishing Co., Inc.

ISBN: 0-440-90837-X

Reprinted by arrangement with Chilton Book Company
Manufactured in the United States of America
First Laurel printing—October 1971
Second Laurel printing—July 1972
Third Laurel printing—July 1973
Fourth Laurel printing—August 1973
Fifth Laurel printing—May 1974
Sixth Laurel printing—December 1974
Seventh Laurel printing—August 1975
Eighth Laurel printing—April 1977
Ninth Laurel printing—June 1978

" 'Anyway, if you think about it, everybody's got the same problem, more or less. I mean, even those who can speak well—without any speech defect, that is.'

'Okay,' he said. 'I give up.'

'One way or another, it's all communication, isn't it? We're all trying to communicate—to break through with somebody—so we can understand them.'

He thought about that and liked it."

But as much as he liked that idea, Roger realized that he was losing a race. He had a harder time breaking through than other people and it might not be long before he'd just not feel like trying anymore.

KIN PLATT has been a cartoonist and worked in newspapers, television, and radio. His other books have included *The Blue Man*, *Big Max* and *Sinbad and Me*, winner of the Edgar award.

THE LAUREL-LEAF LIBRARY brings together under a single imprint outstanding works of fiction and nonfiction particularly suitable for young adult readers, both in and out of the classroom. This series is under the editorship of Charles F. Reasoner, Professor of Elementary Education, New York University.

ALSO AVAILABLE IN THE LAUREL-LIBRARY:

MYSTERY OF THE WITCH WHO WOULDN'T
by Kin Platt

HEY, DUMMY
by Kin Platt

STICKS AND STONES
by Lynn Hall

PISTOL
by Adrienne Richard

FOG
by Mildred Lee

THE YEAR OF THE RACOON
by Lee Kingman

THE PIGMAN
by Paul Zindel

IF I LOVE YOU, AM I TRAPPED FOREVER?
by M. E. Kerr

DINKY HOCKER SHOOTS SMACK!
by M. E. Kerr

*In appreciation to
V. E. Masters
for the love and
understanding and skill
that have given children
a chance at happiness*

THE
BOY
WHO
COULD
MAKE
HIMSELF
DISAPPEAR

CHAPTER ONE

AFTER THE BIG BREAKUP Roger felt that they were waiting for him to say something. Finally it was all decided, without his help. His father moved out of the big house in Brentwood to the beach house in Malibu. There were phone calls and conferences and then a lot of packing and almost before he knew it he was living in New York City with his mother. He was supposed to have a final meeting with his father but a big conference came up with important people who couldn't be kept waiting, his father's secretary explained. He would write Roger immediately. Roger was not to worry.

His mother said, "Well, that's your father for you. Now perhaps you'll understand."

Only he didn't.

He knew it was all over. They weren't ever going to be a big happy family anymore—not that they really

ever had been. But now everyone could tell and it
was definitely final.

He didn't know whether he was supposed to favor
his father or his mother but neither one asked him for
sympathy or affection. Or understanding.

On the silvery jet flying east he was relieved he
hadn't taken sides. It was a little like not having to
take a loyalty oath. He liked them both about equal-
ly, he decided. His father was too busy producing pictures to ever have time to fool around with him, like
some of the other kids' fathers. And his mother seemed
to live in her own world, seeing how many canvases
she could cover with big areas of paint. He was alone
most of the time anyway so it really didn't make too
much difference, he thought. The only trouble was
that even though he understood the situation he still
felt surrounded by a big emptiness, as if he were somewhere out in space. That's why he had wished the
plane could stay up there forever, then maybe he
wouldn't have any more problems.

When he decided to write his father and got out
the paper, he found out it wasn't going to be as easy
as he had imagined to let him know he didn't have
any hard feelings.

Hey, Dad, he wanted to say, *well here we are in
New York City in the new apartment Mom found.
Believe it or not we live on the eighteenth floor. They
have two elevators to take you up and down and four
elevator operators (men) who take turns. Also two
doormen to push the revolving door downstairs in the
lobby.*

My room has a great view of the Hudson River. I

*can see all the way across it to New Jersey. There's a
big sign over there that lights up every night: SPRY.
Then, farther up, to the right, I can see the George
Washington Bridge. That's quite a sight, too, with
millions of cars coming and going. And the same for
the West Side Highway which runs alongside Riverside
Drive right under my window. Almost as busy as the
Freeway only they don't drive as fast here.*

*There was some furniture in the apartment when
we came—I guess it's called a furnished apartment—
and I feel like I'm in somebody else's house visiting,
you know what I mean? My desk is white, kind of
small but okay. There's a white dresser and a mirror
and a white bookcase and they even left some books
behind, girls' books, mysteries. That girl reporter
series, where crimes are always solved right away in
that small town because she's such a great detective.
She thinks.*

*I'll be starting school here in a few days, as soon as
my grades arrive. There's one not too far away, a private one. I don't know any other kids yet but there
must be plenty around.*

He also wanted to write: *Dear Dad, I sure miss you
and all the cigars you used to smoke up the house
with, I mean when you were home weekends, and I
miss the pool and the fruit trees and looking up at
mountains every day and seeing the snow up there
and I'm sorry you and mother broke up.*

But he knew his father was too busy to read all this
junk. Heck, he had this big TV comedy show to put
out every week with that nutty comic, that Jerry
Jeeks. Not to mention the movies he was always pro-

ducing, too; it wasn't easy getting together all the big stars and the director and the writer and the cameraman, worrying about the production running smoothly without any hitches so it would make people laugh and make money at the box office.

Instead, he wrote:

> *Hi Dad, our new place is swell. A 20-story building right next to the Hudson River, and that's more water than we ever had in our back yard (joke). I guess we'll get along fine here. Just send money (joke). Hope you don't let that Jerry Jeeks nut give you your ulcer back. Your loving son, Roger.*

It felt better writing his name, Roger, because he couldn't say it. Not properly. Not without making people laugh or pretend not to.

Not Roger, not Riverside Drive, not Rasputin, not Red Russia, not ringadingding, not any word with an R in it. Here he was he thought, twelve years old, for gosh sakes, still sounding like a little kid with that baby-talk lisp that made all his R's sound like W's.

He looked up from the desk into the mirror.

"My name is Roger Baxter," he said.

It came out Wa-ja.

"Roger," he said, insistently.

"Wa-ja," the boy in the mirror said.

"Roger, Roger," he screamed.

"Wa-ja Wa-ja," the boy inside the mirror yelled back with an angry face.

He crumpled the letter into a ball, threw it furiously at the mirror and watched it bounce off onto the floor. He kicked it away. *What the heck*, he thought. *He doesn't have time to read this anyway. And what's more, he couldn't care less. All I am to him is a skinny kid who's too dumb even to say his own name. As far as he's concerned it's probably good-by, good riddance.*

He got up and walked out into the large rear living room fronting on Riverside Drive. He leaned hard to open the glass door and stepped out upon the small terrace. Thick black bars, sunk a foot apart into the concrete, rose vertically to about five feet over his head. He reached for them, grateful for the cold security that kept him from falling over the edge.

A wave of dizziness swept over him as he looked down at the street far below. Eighteen stories. Wow, what a drop that would be! He shuddered. He imagined himself falling, dropping head over heels, twisting and turning, becoming smaller and smaller and wondered if he'd be screaming. He saw his mouth gaping open but heard no sound. Probably because of the wind nobody would hear him screaming. He saw himself a pinpoint far below, falling like a stone, helpless and trying to put on the brakes, maybe trying to fly by flapping his arms in a last desperate effort. Then, suddenly, the sidewalk and—wham, crunch, splash! Ugh! what a mess. Lucky he didn't fall on a pedestrian come to think of it. Would *that* have been something!

He wondered how many people a year fell off the buildings in New York. Probably lots. Even this building, with a terrace on every floor, must have plenty of accidents. Maybe that old black iron railing wasn't as strong as it looked. Maybe the concrete underneath was rotten or they'd mixed too much sand in it. He moved back a little, putting his weight behind him, holding the bars more lightly now, at arms length. He pushed at them, finally using all his strength. Well, they tested okay but you never know. He decided he'd test them every day just to make sure they were holding up okay. His mother wouldn't ever think of a thing like that. He could see he'd have to do all the worrying around here.

He watched the double line of cars below, strung out like tiny colored bugs pulled on invisible strings. He could hear the steady hum of traffic, the squealing of brakes and tires, the harsh changing of gears as the little sports cars shifted up and down, revving their engines loudly as they zipped around the bigger cars, jockeying for position.

His eyes sought the river and he saw a line of barges moving south, loaded with three freight cars. Hey, what next? he wondered. Then a little tug moved jauntily by, its single funnel coughing black wisps of smoke. He heard it toot as it passed the barges. He wondered why it looked so cheerful and made up his mind to check all other tugs to see if they gave him that same impression.

He was going to give this river a lot of his attention. Probably it would always hold something interesting. He wished right now he could see a big aircraft carrier. His eyes searched far to the right but the Navy was elsewhere.

Then he was staring at the thin arched line that was the George Washington Bridge. It spanned the river gracefully, the little dots of cars moving swiftly along its upper and lower roadbeds. *Plenty of New Jersey commuters,* he thought. *I wonder what it's like over there.* It was about four o'clock in the afternoon and the sun, bright and red on the far shore, hurt his eyes. As he turned away, a glitter of light from a window opposite him caught his attention.

His building was U shaped, divided into two sections. This was the north wing, the 87th Street part. All the terraces faced one another the entire length of the courtyard. He saw hundreds of windows running from top to bottom, most of them with blinds drawn.

The light glittered again. It came from an opposite apartment where the blinds were slightly open. Then they were opened wide, as if by mistake, and as suddenly snapped shut. That seemed peculiar, but the blinds were shut tightly now and he could only wonder, look nonchalant, and turn away. Out of the corner of his eye, he saw the lower blinds being lifted again and a face peering out. The face ducked away out of sight. Then he saw what had caught his eye before; a telescope, a black telescope. That was okay, he thought. He wished he had one himself to better enjoy the view and bring everything on the river clearer and closer.

He started to go inside and only then realized what had bothered him.

Whoever was using the telescope wasn't admiring the view, but watching him!

CHAPTER TWO

"You mean I've got to wear a white shirt and a tie and a jacket? But why?" he asked his mother.

"Because that's the way people dress here, Roger. This is New York."

"I know. But I'm not going any place."

"You don't have to advertise that to the whole world, Roger. Just do as I say. Don't argue."

Well, I guess you'll just have to get used to it, buddy, he told himself. *If it's going to make that much difference, I don't want to be a disgrace to the neighborhood and the house and everything.*

He could never figure out his mother. Artists were supposed to go around not caring what they looked like or where or how they lived. His mother was an artist, or at least always painting pictures, which was the same thing anyway, wasn't it? Only everything had to be just right for her. And it didn't make any difference if you stood on your head; she always got her way after all. Maybe that was why his father always kept himself so busy with making pictures and didn't spend much time at home. It sure avoided a lot of arguments.

He had no idea living in New York would be so different. The first big difference was that everybody walked. They walked fast and they talked fast and they seemed to know exactly what they were doing every minute. He felt almost like some sort of hick from the country. It wasn't that he was slow or stupid. He only felt that way; as if he were on a different time belt, moving at his own slower rate of speed while everybody else whirled past, smiling and glittering and sure of themselves. They were traveling side by side but at different revolutions.

It's like California's the Twilight Zone, he thought.

He had never before seen so many people, so many cars, so many stores and theaters and buildings. The buildings towered all around him, solid, packed with thousands of other beings; and wherever he walked, hundreds of windows winked down, dazzling him with their splintered shafts of reflected sunlight.

The smells and sounds, too, were different. It was like living in another world, a world he was caught up in and would have to learn to live in.

It was always windy at the corner of Riverside Drive and 86th Street, he discovered. Their apartment house straddled the corner and he had to bow his head and fight fierce gusts to reach the revolving glass doors that would spin him into the lobby sparkling-eyed and breathless and feeling as if he'd just won a battle over a giant.

The cool fall wind came in stiff and strong from across the Hudson River, sweeping over the red clay cliffs of New Jersey, whistling a long-held note, rattling the window panes in the big buildings and hotels, blowing the hats off old men and children and sending any newspapers it could find high into the air. It made him feel better to know this wind was only prankish. Back home in Southern California, where he'd lived all his life, the wind this time of year was feared. They called it the Santa Ana.

Also the Devil Winds.

When the heat and low humidity made the Los Angeles hills drier than a desert, then the devil winds swept in, hot and parching. They swept across the dried and crackling chaparral, the sumac and wild lilac, breathing hotly on the brush, exploding it finally into flame. Then it would whip up the flame, driving with incredible speed across the spiny ridges and canyons, making it hedgehop across streets, leap from rooftop to rooftop, snapping and popping, roaring like a locomotive, driving the people out of their hill homes in their pajamas and house coats, carrying pictures, odd pieces of furniture, clothing, whatever they thought worth saving. That wind blew freakish and gusty, sending up towering jagged arrows of flame and swirling clouds of smoke, turning the borate bombers and the fire fighters into helpless haggard smoke-grimed men.

Their big house in Brentwood, in West Los Angeles, had been spared by the last big fire he'd seen but some of their neighbors had not been as fortunate. It was as if the fire were playing eeny meeny miney moe, picking on sudden impulse which house to devour. The flat wood-shingled roofs made it easier to pick and choose and the people watched red-eyed and frightened the awful game of leap frog.

Roger could still smell that last fire, still see the rabbits and raccoons that came out of the hills shrouded in smoke, the fawn that walked dazedly right down his street and stood on his lawn quivering. People were stumbling out of their houses carrying crazy things, one woman a tennis racket and a mink coat. That was Mrs. Ferguson. He didn't even know she played tennis.

His mother had all her paintings out on the grass— he'd helped her carry some of the larger ones—and it looked as if she were having an exhibition. She'd even put some into the station wagon before the wind and flames danced over another hill. A lot of the other kids were standing on their roofs, wetting them down with garden hoses.

"You'd only fall off," his mother had told him. "You stay around here where I might need you."

Apart from asking him to help her bring out the big paintings, she never did.

If only he could have made the fawn understand . . .

"Look," he wanted to say, "there's nothing to worry about any more. See? The fire's going the other way. There's a road going through up there and in a little while the fire fighters will have it under control."

But the fawn only stood there with glazed eyes and shivering twitching limbs, his spotted flanks shining wet with sweat. He looked dead tired.

Everybody else was acting as if at a carnival, yelling encouragement to the fire fighters, whooping when the fire leaped, groaning or screaming when it reached out hot flickering fingers of flame to the shingled roofs, rushing in and out of houses with the first thing that came to hand, back inside again for something more important.

Nobody saw the fawn standing there shaking and terribly tired. Nobody but Roger.

He wanted to throw his arms around the fawn's neck and hug him but the fawn looked so nervous Roger was afraid he would bolt.

"It's okay," he whispered. "It's okay now. Honest. You can twust me." He stood perfectly still, wanting to be closer but, knowing the shyness of wild things, not daring to move. He waited, trying to tell the fawn with his eyes that he could be trusted. *I'm his only friend up here,* he thought. *He's got to trust me. Please trust me, fawn.*

The fire was crackling and popping and hissing farther over the canyon hill now, disappearing at times in a great pall of smoke. There were exultant cries from the roof hosers and observers in trees. Far overhead a police helicopter dangled, its rotor blades whirling and crashing, hanging fishtailed there as if suspended somehow in the sky.

The freakish wind suddenly shifted again and black billows of smoke swirled back. The little knots of people in front of their homes screamed and rushed in and out again, holding all their arms could carry.

"Don't yell so," Roger wanted to tell them. "You'll frighten my fawn." He glared at them, his jaws tight with anger.

The fawn looked at Roger. It was as if he had asked a question. Roger's heart pounded.

"Wait he-ah," he whispered. "I'll get some. Please don't go away."

He brought some water back in a basin. He carried it carefully, levelly, not wanting to spill a single drop. He set it down about five feet away from the fawn, trying not to have the basin scrape harshly on the concrete of the patio. Then he straightened up and stepped back, aware now that he was shaking and trembling himself.

"Okay, fawn," he whispered. "Help ya self."

The fawn watched him steadily for a long moment.

His long ears twitched forward, then flicked back. The long graceful neck arched and he stood motionless, his moist brown eyes staring. Then the long slender head dipped and the fawn was lapping the water, delicately, deliberately. It was as if he had all the time in the world and his lungs weren't hot and parched. His slim legs were spread, forelegs canted in the odd angle that seemed an awkward pose for an animal with such grace.

I wonder if he always stands that way when he drinks. What can I feed him? He's probably starved. What do fawns eat anyway? Some kind

of greens, maybe? Berries? We've got some straw-
berries inside. Will he take them from me? May-
be he can't spare the time.

The fawn seemed to read his mind. His head
came up suddenly and he gave Roger another
long deliberate stare. Then his nostrils, damp and
velvety, quivered. His neck stretched and his head
turned to follow the fire high in the hills.

He struck the stone of the terrace with his
hooves. Then, almost before Roger knew it, he
was walking silently across the lawn.

"No," he whispered, shaking his head helplessly, "don't go yet. It's still awfully hot back theh.
And theh's an awful lot of smoke."

The great eyes were on his face again, staring.
It's as if he's looking right through me, Roger
shivered. Now the small extended head of the
deer dipped twice, as if in salute. His legs quivered.
He walked unsteadily toward the hedge in the
side garden, head up high now, the black nostrils
searching and sniffing. Then his haunches were
somehow gathered, trembling, and he was soaring
over the high hedge in a long graceful leap that
seemed as if it would never end. Directly ahead
of him hung the dark ugly pall of smoke that
blanketed the forest beyond the hill.

"No," Roger wanted to cry, "don't go back
there. It's still not safe. Everything's blistering
hot. You'll burn your feet."

His eyes searched and strained against the curling wreaths of smoke but the fawn disappeared as
silently as he had come. *Maybe he has family*

back there. That's probably it. His family is lost back there in those charred woods and he can't stand that. He's going back even if it's to die there.

He waited all night at the window, head pressed against the cold pane, staring into the dark shadows. Finally, stiff and cold, he had to get into his bed, a terrible fear gripping him, making his teeth chatter.

Well, I tried, fawn, but the trouble is, I know you're not coming back.

CHAPTER THREE

HE SPENT a lot of time going up and down the elevators in the big building overlooking the drive. The cars were automatic and Roger wondered why they needed men to run them when anyone could operate them by merely pressing down the little black buttons, each with a numeral in white on it, indicating the floor. The twentieth floor had no number but was marked PH. It took him a long time to find out those letters meant penthouse, a special rooftop garden apartment leased by a very beautiful model whom he had never seen.

There were two other buttons with letters instead of numbers. There was a B, for basement and an L for laundry. He found himself sometimes idly wishing that one of the buttons had an R for Roger. Then everyone would know his name without him having to pronounce it. Why couldn't he have been named something simple like Huey? That would have been a cinch. Or Bill. Or Pen. Even Otto would have been okay. No, it had to be something with an R in it. Like Roger. Whoever would have thought a name could so torment a person? A name you couldn't pronounce. A name you couldn't even spell because of that stupid R.

Roger shifted his school books from his right arm to his left but the outside doorman beat him to the revolving doors.

"Yes, sir," he said cheerfully, giving the doors a hearty push. "And how are you today, sir?"

"Fine," said Roger. He was annoyed without exactly knowing why. Perhaps it was being called "sir." Were they kidding? Also, he liked to push his own revolving doors. He hardly ever got a chance, with those doormen leaping to their doors like robots whenever he appeared, beating him to it.

He walked across the glass-walled marble lobby hearing the crystal chandeliers tinkle high above as the wind stirred them. The elevator car was waiting, door open. Roger stepped inside and nodded to the operator. It was George, the afternoon man. There was also a morning man, an evening man, and a night man. The last one worked the early morning hours of two-to-six and could usually be found outside the car, asleep in a wicker chair. He told everyone he went to night school and this made the late crowd tolerant; nobody wanted to be harsh with a student who couldn't stay awake. Roger thought he was kind of old to still be a student.

"Eighteen, please," Roger said to George, the afternoon man.

"Yes, sir, I know. You're the new boy, aren't you? Baxter?"

"Uh-huh," said Roger, noticing another passenger in the car.

"What's your name again?"

"Roger," he wanted to say but he tightened his mouth and pretended he hadn't heard.

The other passenger was a dark-haired girl. She smelled of sweet flowers and lemons, all mixed up, and looked as if she had just walked off one of the pages of those fashion magazines his mother read. She leaned with easy grace against the opposite corner of the car and looked at him with a casual indifference. She was the most beautiful live girl he had ever seen, he decided. She was so tall he had to look up beyond his lashes to see the top of her head. Her eyes were a dark violet, heavily fringed with thick black lashes incredibly long. Her face was a glowing pale white oval against the jet blackness of her hair. She had a string of pearls at the throat of her black dress. Her fur coat was open and he thought she was very thin and probably froze in this weather.

The elevator man didn't give up. "What's your name again?" he asked doggedly.

Roger took a deep breath. Here it was again. When you least expected it. The red indicator lights were flashing the floors and he kept his eyes fixed on them. Thirteen, fourteen, fifteen, sixteen.

He felt the pressure building up in the silence of the car but he waited a little longer. Then he said in a low voice: "You guessed it befaw. Bax-ta."

He held his breath, waiting, letting his head slump

back against the cool metallic wall of the car. He looked up at the vividly beautiful, softly contoured face of the tall girl, trying to act nonchalant. She nodded her head, almost imperceptibly. Then, suddenly, incredibly, she closed one eye and winked at him. A slight smile edged the bright red line of her lips.

What a cool girl, he thought. She put herself right on his side without even knowing what the battle was all about. He couldn't wink back and spoil the game. Instead he sniffed and cleared his throat. The elevator doors slid open with a whoosh and a bang. He wanted to act cool, too, going out.

"Well, so long," he said to the girl, not daring to look at her again. His chest felt tight with excitement.

" 'By doll," she said, her voice low and with a curious huskiness.

The back of George's neck was red as he walked out. Well, Roger thought, his jaw line tight, that would teach him to be such a wise guy. Asking him that dumb question—as if he didn't know the name. That's all he had to do, say "Wa-ja" before that tall slim girl with the inscrutable smile of an Egyptian princess. He never would have dared to look at her again.

18 G where he lived was directly opposite the shaft of the elevator, so Roger made a show of whistling and jangling his keys as he approached his door. But the doors of the elevator had already slid shut and the car gone on up. *Up where?* he wondered. The next instant he knew. The top button. PH—the garden penthouse of the beautiful model! It *had* to be her! Wow!

A new feeling of elation over the encounter carried him on air across the threshold. He let the door slam without caring. He didn't put the safety chain up over the door or double lock it, either. What was there to worry about, anyway?

A note on the dining room table from his mother said she had to go to some art galleries and might be a little late. And if he got hungry he could make himself a sandwich.

The kitchen was a mess. There was a stack of dishes and pots and pans a foot high in the sink. *I guess she sure had to leave in a hurry*, he thought.

Roger poked his head inside the big white refrigerator. Then, after a moment, he closed it. *Make a sandwich out of what?* he wondered disgustedly. They didn't have a maid around anymore and he had an uneasy foreboding of taking pot luck in the kitchen from now on. Without his father around maybe his mother didn't have to go through the motions any longer.

What happened about money now? He knew his father made a lot but the arrangements were never disclosed to him. He was pretty sure they wouldn't go down the drain completely and be charity cases or beggars or anything. But he experienced the first stirring of curiosity about how things were going to be from now on.

He wondered whose fault it really was. Divorces didn't just happen, did they? And yet the strange thing, the thing that bothered him most, was having no warning of the break-up. He felt a little cheated that it had all happened so easily. Did they suddenly decide one morning at breakfast, "Hey—let's get this thing over with. Okay?"

Or maybe it was done with a phone call. "Hello, Philip? This is Connie. I've just decided this marriage is for the birds. Shall we call it a day? You agree? By all means. Yes. Thank you very much. Good-by. Are you coming home for dinner? Oh. Well, good-by."

Or did his dad tell his mother that *he* was fed up. And if he were, Roger wondered, fed up with what?

What?

What went on all the time that he didn't know about? What happened? It wasn't *his* fault, was it? Baby talk wasn't the end of the world. It wasn't like having cancer or anything. Even that moron Jerry Jeeks got a lot of laughs with his crazy way of talking.

What happened—so that one day he could be part of a family in a nice big solid house, and the next day it was heigh-ho off we go to the big city three thousand miles away eighteen stories up in the sky in a house with a thousand other people living in it? It was spooky.

Maybe it was the California climate or something. Almost every other kid he knew out there had a second father or mother, and some were going on their third. Peter Brook had had four fathers already and he was only nine. That was the record as far as Roger knew.

Well, let's face it, he told himself. *You're liable to be next, buddy. One of these days you'll wake up and say "hi" to a new dad. One you never saw before and can't even imagine right now. Maybe, for all you*

*know, it'll be like out there in California and he'll
have a few kids of his own. From another marriage, or
two. There'll be visiting day and visiting privileges,
like they do; and every week or every other, depend-
ing, there'll be this kid, or maybe even a couple of
them, that he has to take out and show a good time
to. Only this time it would be as part of the family.
Your family.*

*For all you know, Roger Baxter, Wa-ja Baxter—who-
ever you are—you'll be coming down soon with a sister
or a brother. Not bad for an only child, huh?*

It seemed as if everybody out there on the West
Coast got tired of each other every couple of years. It
was like trading in your old car. He didn't know too
much about New Yorkers yet, but practically every
kid he'd met so far had the same father or mother
that he was born with. Barring accidents, that was.
Not that they were all exactly crazy about their situation either, he'd found out. Some kids with mean
ones for parents wished sometimes for some kind of
change, even would be willing to take pot luck, and
not just in the refrigerator.

He threw his school books down on his bed but was
too keyed up to start his homework. Instead, he
walked out to the big living room picture window,
parted the drapes, and stared down at the river. The
sky was the color of slate and on the water the wind
ruffled the little whitecaps that chased each other all
the way across from the Jersey side. The window was
cold. All the nice feeling he had brought into the
apartment was going fast. On the terrace he could
watch the traffic-stream of cars. Maybe he'd see some-

thing down there to cheer him up again. Maybe the telescope peeper would be operating again and he'd unravel that mystery.

He stood outside wrapped in a mantle of cool air, listening to the muted sounds of traffic far below. He felt somehow as if he were on a cloud. Roger Baxter, high up on a cloud, where nobody could reach him, where he could stand without falling through its fleecy softness, riding it like a Viking rode the waves, tall, straight and unafraid. He would discover new worlds, meet strange people with languages he could listen to without worrying over meaning, who if he told them his name was Wa-ja, wouldn't even know the difference. Why not? he thought. It could be like Will or Wally or Werner. Nobody cared if *they* started with W's, and girls had chances at Winnie and Wilma and Wendy. It was too bad some wise guy had made up the rules. Like everything had to be just so.

He was staring boldly at the drawn blinds across the courtyard. *Come on, let's get it over with. Are we peeping today or not?* As if in answer one of the blinds halfway down was lifted cautiously, the thin white slat angled at one end.

Roger snorted contemptuously: *Come on, take a good look, whoever you are.*

Then the center blinds lifted slightly and he thought he glimpsed a small white hand and long yellow hair but he couldn't be sure because of the distance.

The blinds dropped. After a few minutes Roger felt foolish standing there on the stone terrace, staring. What if he'd been wrong the first time? Maybe he just imagined he saw a telescope. Just like he imagined now he'd seen a girl.

The chill of the afternoon air made him turn to go inside. Just then he was certain the blinds across the way were suddenly drawn apart. But he refused to look back, storming inside his apartment and slamming the terrace door.

"We got a long lease here," he muttered. "I'll find out *some* day!"

CHAPTER FOUR

MR. RAWLING was a tartar to most of the students at the Busby School. To Roger he was something more: an enigma. A painful one.

Roger had never before met any person with such a strangely commanding personality. And, since Mr. Rawling was not only his home room but his English teacher, Roger had a lot of time to try to get used to him. But it was like trying to hold quicksilver. The form kept changing, running away from him.

Mr. Rawling had once been an actor. In the teaching profession he held on to his histrionics, constructing ordinary sentences somehow in high drama, posturing and mincing and clowning shamelessly to get the effect he sought. He used his voice as an instrument, with almost surgical skill flaying, probing, cutting and dissecting his subjects. So cleverly contrived were his stagings that his classes were always audiences rather than groups of students. Mr. Rawling was the whole show, always on stage, always the star. And with the sure instinct of a gifted performer, he knew when a mollifying quip was needed to soothe the unfortunates pierced with his wit and his sarcasm.

He was slender, of medium height, ascetic and good looking enough to make girl students dreamily sigh and tremble when he strode into the classroom. Their spirits rose and fell according to his disposition, while he charmed and goaded them into an education. When he put a carelessly graceful hand to his wavy blond hair while addressing them, a shudder almost visibly engulfed them. He looked down with eyes as blue and cold as agate, his thin lips curled in disdain, and they awaited his remarks with a mixture of terror and love, unable to move while being prepared for their morning lesson.

Roger was far removed from such worship.

From his very first day at Busby, he somehow knew his survival there depended upon how he could counter whatever happened to be the current whim of Mr. Rawling. For such a contest he felt hopelessly ill equipped and outclassed. He had difficulty pronouncing Mr. Rawling's name and none of his evasions served him.

"My name is Rawling," the teacher said to Roger. "Now there's no point to my being Rawling if you persist in calling me something else, is there?" His voice was framed in kindliness and polite inquiry.

"No," said Roger. He was standing near his desk chair, his legs suddenly quivering and trembling convulsively. *Like my fawn,* he instantly thought. Safe in school, what the heck did he have to be scared about?

The soothing voice of Mr. Rawling continued. "Now if my name were Armand Jean du Plessis de Richelieu, or Nikolai Andreevich Rimski-Korsakov, or Maximilien François Marie Isidore de Robespierre —I could possibly understand your having a little difficulty pronouncing it." The class had started to titter. Mr. Rawling, leaning back indolently in his chair, pretended to ignore it. "But Rawling is such a simple name. Don't you think?"

Roger didn't answer. A sticky hotness swept his face and his hair went damp. Everyone's eyes were on him, he knew, all strangers' eyes. The tittering started again, then a girl in the back row suddenly, uncontrollably, shrieked.

"Hardly *that* funny, Miss Wide-in-the-Beam," said Mr. Rawling, a sneer curling his lips.

Roger didn't look back to see the discomfited Miss Wide-in-the-Beam. He was grateful for the side-tracking of Mr. Rawling yet sorry for her, too, as the room shrilled with laughter at her expense. Was she really "wide-in-the-beam" and if so how could the teacher kid about a thing like that in front of everybody?

Mr. Rawling clapped his hands for attention. The laughter slowly subsided until the room was almost still, then another girl seated to Roger's left let out another squeal and was helplessly lost in laughter.

"You're hardly one to call the kettle black, Miss Tight-Pants," Mr. Rawling snapped.

Roger could see this new victim, to whom the

jibe didn't seem as important as being the center of
attention.

Feeling that the teacher's attack upon him was
now finished, Roger sank slowly into his seat and,
when Mr. Rawling appeared to take no notice, leaned
back breathing a deep sigh of relief.

The teacher's low conversational voice got off a
few other quips, evidently personal allusions also, because the class guffawed, turned heads, and some kids
pretended to fall off their chairs. The coughing and
stamping of feet subsided into spasmodic giggles, the
girls fingering their hair and the boys fidgeting. Roger
stayed unsmiling.

When there was complete silence, Mr. Rawling
tipped his chair back, lips pursed, moodily surveying
the room. "Now, then, where was I?" he plaintively
asked, looking bewildered and lost, and Roger knew
the attack was far from over. The knuckles of his
hand whitened from gripping the polished desk arm.

"Oh, yes," he heard Mr. Rawling say. "We were
discussing clarity of language, weren't we?"

The class murmured assent.

"You see, Roger," Mr. Rawling continued, "English is a very precise language. The King's English
means just that. Language fit for a king. We have
mutterers and mumblers enough. Each word is precious
for meaning, each syllable, each letter. That is why I
am pursuing this at length with you now. The fact
that I insist upon proper enunciation of my name is
hardly cause for hilarity"—Mr. Rawling glared fake-
fiercely toward the rear section of the class and Roger

hoped that Miss Wide-Beam would not lose control of herself again. "What we need desperately today is the ability to communicate—I cannot emphasize that strongly enough—to insure *that* we must have proper speech. Proper grammar, proper syntax, proper enunciation—"

"Oh, boy," thought Roger, "here we go again."

He heard Mr. Rawling's voice farther away now, but still plaintive, still querulous. "Have you ever thought about doing anything regarding your speech defect, Baxter?"

Boy, have I! You'd never guess!

"I think I'll write a note." Mr. Rawling started to scribble on a desk pad. "And I suggest you take this directly to Miss Clemm after class, during your study period." He continued writing. "Dr. Clemm is very good at this sort of thing," he said.

His voice was very far away now; fading, fading into other voices . . .

One was that teacher, that speech therapist in California school. Miss Madison. But she had such a *soft* voice.

"Rowf!" Miss Madison was roaring at him. "You have to pretend you're a dog, Roger. Growl! Growl, Roger. Like this—*rowf! rowf! rowf!*"

Her large blue eyes weren't nearly pretty any more, as he stiffened against the wall watching her, watching the growling of that pretty woman who had deceived him.

Roger was nine years old when he came home one day and announced he wasn't going to school any more.

"Theh a bunch of wats," he said.

"Wats?" asked his mother.

"Oh, you know," said Roger.

"Do you mean rats?" asked his father, who happened to be home, sitting at the table.

"That's wight," said Roger.

Mr. Baxter sighed, "I wish you'd try to pronounce your R's," he said almost petulantly. "I'm sure you could learn to if you tried. Do you want to go through your whole life talking baby talk?"

Now what kind of a dumb question is that? Tears of anger and frustration flooded Roger's eyes. *What's the matter with him? Don't he know* anything?

"That's what I'm talking about," he shrilled. "What do you think I'm talking about, you dope!"

"Roger, that is not a nice way to talk to your father," Mrs. Baxter said. "Now apologize."

"I won't, I won't," he yelled almost hysterically. "Theh a bunch of wats and she lied to me."

"Who lied to you?" asked his mother.

"Miss Cweepy blue eyes, that's who," he yelled.

"Who?" asked his father.

"You'd know who if you wo-ant so busy always jumping to the phone for that dopey mo-won you wo'k fo-ah!"

"If you're referring to Jerry Jeeks, he happens

to be the nation's number one comic," replied his father, "and furthermore, if I happen to be on the phone with him a lot it's only because he needs me." His father's voice was very patient.

"You've got ya own baby," yelled Roger and was instantly sorry.

"What Roger is saying, dear, is that he has been going to a special speech-therapy class at school to try to learn to speak correctly."

"Don't tell him," raged Roger. "Let him guess!"

"Oh?" said his father. "Have you? Well, that's nice. Very nice. I think you ought to keep it up." He put his newspaper down on the table. "Now if you all will excuse me, I have to make some phone calls."

"Tell him I said he's a dopey mo-won," Roger called after him.

Mrs. Baxter rang the little bell for the maid to clear the table. "Why do you say he's a moron?" she asked Roger.

"Because he is. Any dope who makes fun of sick kids, is."

Not only that kind, he reminded himself. How about the other kind? The kind that weren't dopes and you could tell right away and yet they cheated you anyway. There ought to be some kind of law, he thought, to make people wear signs telling exactly what kind of people they were. Then everybody would know and there wouldn't be any trouble.

He had been going to that special speech class

for several weeks and making progress. The
teacher in charge—was she a doctor? he wondered—was a kind-looking soft-spoken woman
who approached Roger with large concerned
eyes.

"I'm certain you can learn to talk properly,"
she said in her gentle voice, "just like other
children."

She didn't ask him if that wasn't what he
wanted, wasn't it? Like the other dopes he'd been
meeting. Her mouth was small and firm, her eyes
the blue of the sky he saw over him every day.
She wasn't too young any more, he noticed, but
she acted young.

Like the way she stooped to pick up the
blocks.

"You can do whatever you want to here," she
said. "You can throw these blocks around if you'd
like to."

"Why would I want to do that?" asked Roger.

Miss Madison shrugged her slight shoulders.
"Some children like to," she murmured. Her
voice was so soft you could hardly hear it. Too
bad she's got crooked teeth in front, Roger
thought, though they're good and white anyway.

"That's why we have this special room for children," Miss Madison was saying. "In case they
feel like breaking something, we understand and
they don't get blamed."

Roger looked around the room. It was small
and had very little furniture in it, just a low
chair for kids and a small sort of work table

with different kinds of blocks on it and a lot of
that paint you smeared on with your fingers and
even after you washed it off right away, like the
jar said, you couldn't wash off the smell—only
they didn't mention that, he noticed.

The only wall with any kind of decoration had
just a big wide kind of gray mirror in it. He
couldn't see himself in it unless he stood on his
toes.

"Okay," said Roger. "I'll bwake something if
you want me to. What do you want me to
bwake?"

Miss Madison smiled around her crooked
teeth.

"That's entirely up to you, Roger. Whatever
you like."

"How about that mih-wuh?" He raised himself
on his toes and saw himself clearly in the mirror,
but very gray.

Miss Madison didn't look the least bit alarmed.

"That might be kind of expensive to replace,"
she said. "And besides, why would you want to
break a silly old mirror?"

"Because it's all gway," said Roger.

"Maybe it can't help it," she said softly and
Roger was pleased with that idea.

She squatted suddenly on her haunches, peering into a pile of junky stuff on the floor in the
corner. "I think we still have some tin soldiers
left, if you care to break them."

"I don't have to bwake anything," he said.
"That's kid stuff."

"I didn't say you *had* to," she reminded him. She took his hand and indicated the small chair near her. He guessed she wanted him to sit down and, because she was good and kind and he didn't want to have a tug of war with her about it, he sat down. When she released his hand he missed the soft firm pressure of her fingers. They were strong for a girl, he thought.

"Did you know," she said, "that people who can't pronounce their R's just have lazy tongues? That's all it is."

"Weally?"

Her smile was gentle. "Weally," she said.

He grinned. "You got a lazy tongue."

"I know," she said. "But I'll get better."

He nodded glumly, and she added quickly: "And so will you, Roger."

"It's okay with me," he said.

Boy, wouldn't that be swell? Pop would sure get a kick out of it. He's sure getting fed up with this baby talk by now.

Miss Madison was standing sideways to him now, leaning slightly over. "Can you growl like a dog?"

Roger thought he could.

"Let me hear," she said. "Okay, dog. Growl!"

Roger did his dog growl imitation.

"That's whimpering, Roger, not growling. I want to hear a real mean old dog. Growl like a mean old dog now. Put your chin out. Like this."

Roger looked at her out-thrust chin as she growled. She looked like an English bulldog now, not at all like a gentle, pretty woman. Her light eyebrows came down low over her eyes and her lower lip was pushed forward. He saw a lot more crooked teeth there.

"R-r-r-r—gr-r-r!" said Miss Madison. "Now you, Roger."

"Woo woo woo," he said.

"Say *roof*," she said.

"Woof."

"Say *red*."

"Wed."

"What's your name?"

"You know my name," he said. "I can't say it."

He was telling Adam, a friend of his, about it a few days later.

"You should have broke the mirror when you had the chance," Adam said.

"Why?" Roger asked. They were walking along the outer rim of the canyon and he didn't have to get home for several hours yet.

"Because that's where all the big-shot doctors sit behind, watching you," the other boy said. "Taking notes."

Roger was mystified.

"Behind the mih-wuh?"

Adam snorted. "No, you dope. In the other *room*, behind the mirror. It's like built into the wall. It's one of those trick ones where they can look in from the other side and see you. Only you can't see them because they don't want you to. You see yourself instead."

He felt sick. "Are you positive, Adam?"

"Why do you think it's gray? Did you ever see a gray mirror before, you dope?"

Roger thought about it and about what that nice Miss Madison had said. What was it again? "Maybe it can't help it." Wasn't that what she said?

"*You positive?*" he asked again, shaking and hurting all over.

"Of course. My big sister did that for a hundred years before she finally got married. I remember she told us all about it. They got those same mirrors in department stores to watch people who like to steal things. Don't you know anything?"

That's why she wanted me to sit in the chair, Roger thought fiercely. *I'm glad I didn't growl like a dog, the way she wanted. She couldn't make me. All that bull about lazy tongues. Yeah, sure. You bet. She wanted me to growl like a dog and I didn't. That'll fix her, the big rotten show-off!*

Then he was running as fast as he could, feeling his chest tight around him. He stumbled blindly into a bush, recoiling instantly as the twigs lashed across his face. He swerved abruptly and ran hard again, up the hill, his feet hammering the ground as hard as he could make them.

"Hey, where do you think you're going?" he heard Adam yell.

"Woof woof," he answered. "That's weh, you dope."

CHAPTER FIVE

A SLIM GIRL with long blond hair was passing the door as he came out of the principal's office. She stopped and shook her head when she saw him.

"Too bad about that, before. He's a devil. A real sadist, you know."

Roger wasn't quite sure what a sadist was but it sounded like it fit Mr. Rawling. "I guess so," he said, wondering who she was. *Well, she must be in your class, you dope,* he told himself. *How else would she know what went on?*

"Ugh! He's just awful," she said, tossing her hair. There was something familiar about that long blond hair and suddenly he thought he knew.

"Hey, how's the peeping?" he asked.

Her slightly slanted green eyes opened wider. "What?"

"You know. The telescope peeping," he said.

Her expression was blank. "What telescope peeping? What are you talking about?"

He tried to smile. "I wecognize yuh, heh. Don't you live in that big white building?"

She stamped a black shoe. "Well, yes. I live in a big white building. So what?"

"The one on 87th Stweet and Wiverside Dwive?"

"No, smartie. The one at 79th and Madison." She was looking at him as if he was some kind of an escaped nut.

"I'm sorry," he wanted to say, sweating and hating himself for being such a dope, but her red skirt had already swished angrily past him and her echoing heels reminded him he was alone in the long marble corridor.

Now why did I do a dumb thing like that? he fretted. *The first person in New York to say a kind word to me and I have to louse it up.* He wanted to run after her and tell her he was sorry. *Forget it,* he told himself; *you'll only make things worse.*

How? Things are bad enough already.

Don't worry, you'll find a way.

One thing he was pretty sure of: Mr. Rawling, that sneaky sadist, wasn't going to call this girl any Miss Wide-in-the-Beam or Miss Tight-Pants. He'd have to lie to do it. And if he did, she'd probably murder him.

He went slowly back along the corridor wondering what this nice tempestuous girl's name was. His own temper and red rages left him spent and breathless, so Roger appreciated the controlled fire in her. Telling that kind of girl she was a peeper! What a goof!

He never could save his own tantrums for some-

thing important, something special maybe, nor did he
ever really know what triggered the sputtering and the
sparks, like firecrackers reacting to a lit fuse.

*I guess that's why they always have to punish me.
Like that last time in assembly in that other school in
California . . .*

Roger was seated more than halfway back in
the large auditorium but he could see the anger
in Mr. Wilshire's round face, the beefy redness
of his neck, and the way the principal's right
hand was curled into a fist.

"Someone has thrown a cruller on the wall
in the school cafeteria. I want the person who did
that to stand up!"

There were two other teachers on the plat-
form. On the wall over their heads was the American flag. When the tittering started, like Mr. Wilshire they pretended they didn't hear it, Mrs.
Richie lifting her eyes solemnly up to the flat,
Mrs. Applegate looking down at her shoes.

The two hundred kids in the auditorium were
enjoying this special report about the cruller,
but nobody stood up. Who'd be such a dope?

Roger knew that George Semple had thrown the
cruller at another kid, Henry Allen, who ducked.
It hit the wall and spattered a few of the kids
with creamy filling. George only wasted a fifteen
cent cruller with a bad shot.

"All right," said Mr. Wilshire when the silence
was complete. "We'll try it again. I want the
person who threw that cruller to stand up."

Roger couldn't understand what all the fuss was about. It was only a cruller, for God's sakes. He hadn't even eaten his. He could feel it still in his pocket, soggier than ever. The way he felt now, he wasn't sure that he would *ever* eat it.

The kids stared back defiantly at Mr. Wilshire. He started to sweat, and mop the back of his neck and his head. "All right," he said, "since the guilty party isn't man enough to admit it, I'm afraid we'll all just have to stay right here until he does."

Everyone groaned. Mr. Wilshire yelled for quiet. He probably knew about the big basketball game this afternoon, Roger thought, knew that some of the team were in the auditorium and that they would miss it and the game be forfeited to the rival San Fernando school.

It's not fair, Roger thought. *It's not fair. All because of a crummy cruller on the wall.*

Come on, George. Get up and say you did it. He'll be so relieved, you getting him off the hook, he won't even do anything. Then we can all go see the game. Come on, George,—Be a Hero!

But George just sat there, slouched down in his seat.

There had been a lot of kids in the school cafeteria when George missed Henry so it wasn't any real big secret. But there were still plenty who hadn't been there. He watched the turning heads and heard the whispers as the word passed along: he even began to feel a little proud of everybody for not giving George away.

Then one said: "He ought to get up. Why should we all pay just because he wanted to be a wise guy? I think he's afraid. Just look at him trying to hide back there."

Oh, for Pete's sake, Roger thought.

More heads turned. George's defiant look had faded a little, and his eyes were frightened despite his slight remaining smirk.

He's scared, you dopes, Roger fretted, starting to to rage inside. *Who wouldn't be? But let's keep his secret, huh? You all know what George looks like, for God's sake. He hasn't changed any in the last ten minutes. If you want to look at him, you got all day. Even that dumb Mr. Wilshire is bound to catch on and get wise this way.*

The tide shifted back again to defiance of the principal. Feet started stamping, swelling in volume, the rhythmic beat somehow carrying its own terror. A few whistling catcalls and razzing for the principal from some in the rear of the room openly mocked him now.

This was too much, Roger knew. Real dopey. Was it worth it? He was beginning to get a little confused. But then there was the game, too. Was that so important or was it the unfairness? The grown-up unfairness again.

He saw Mr. Wilshire's look hardening into lines of hatred. He would have to show them he was boss now.

Why did *they* always expect you to give in when *they* issued a command, even when *they* were wrong? Just because *they* were bigger and stronger, or *maybe* knew more?

It was like his mother telling him to put on his sweater because it was cold outside when it wasn't.

It was like his father telling him he couldn't wear his hair long and shaggy like the other kids, punishing him by cutting it all off himself, making him stay in his room for a week, allowing no playtime and no TV either. He remembered storming downstairs the last night of his confinement. A big Jerry Jeeks coast to coast TV show was on and hearing that lisping, nasal, baby-talking voice he hated and the roaring laughter of the studio audience, he threw his shoe right through the TV set, right through that dopey moron Jerry Jeeks' dopey head.

He wanted to get up now and shout that Mr. Wilshire and the prim teachers were acting just like the Nazis, who shot up and buried a whole town for the offense of one single person. He was seeing everybody in assembly as through a filter, their faces shadowed, distorted and ugly. Looking at George he saw that George couldn't care less if everybody stayed after school and was punished forever to pay for his being such a creepy coward. He suddenly lost whatever sympathy he had for George. There would always be some George, hiding while innocent people suffered.

On the stage Mr. Wilshire seemed to Roger to be swaying in a misty reddish light. He blinked and tried to shake the shimmering red sensation out of his eyes and head. The two teachers under the flag were silently pleading with Mr. Wilshire to do something, for God's sakes, while the scattered snickers and growls formed one single concerted noise that rose and fell in swelling waves.

The principal, a little frightened himself, stared down at the two teachers and shrugged, dangling sweaty palms. Then, as if realizing it was now or never, he took a deep breath and with his legs in a wide straddle thrust his bullet head down and raised a clenched fist, holding the pose like a statue until the students' resolve suddenly collapsed.

"Just for that display," he roared, "I'm going to—"

But Roger was on his feet and in his right hand the soggy doughnut saved in his pocket for dividing with the evening birds on the way home up the canyon. A roaring sputtering sound issued from deep in his throat, a groaning kind of screaming that came hoarsely through his clenched teeth as if he were some kind of monster out of a horror picture.

The next instant with sidearm motion, he hurled the cruller, scaling it as if it were a flat stone over water, not consciously aimed at Mr. Wilshire. But it whizzed at his head. Instinctively, he threw his hands in front of his face and ducked. The cruller, rising in erratic flight, soared overhead as the two lady teachers shrieked and cowered, finally coming to a spattering smacking halt right in the middle of the stars and stripes.

Oh, no. Now look what they made me do! They got me dirtying up the American flag with the ooky dribble of a miserable cruller. Just because some big fat bullying old dope had to show he was boss. And because some scared kid couldn't take what was coming to him.

It didn't make sense.

But the expression he saw on George Semple's face did. A look of supreme relief had replaced the fear there. His eyes rolled mockingly to Roger's and his thin lips curled in amused contempt.

"Sucker," George Semple said.

CHAPTER SIX

HE LIVED in a world of words.

Words that asked or begged. Words that pleased. Words that insisted or commanded. Words that described or protested or complained or showed off.

Everybody spoke, it seemed to Roger, as easily and effortlessly as blinking an eye. They spoke torrents of words, all without strain or anxiety. How did they do it?

How come everyone has the magic mouth but me?

You asked people questions and they gave you answers. Or they asked you questions and you were supposed to give *them* answers. People revealed themselves by the way they talked. When you talked then you knew you were somebody. *When you talked then you knew you were still there and you weren't going to disappear.*

When you talked people listened.

Only they didn't have the Jonah words to worry about.

Today I won't say bread or brain or robber or crown or red rose or train or rock and roll or scrape or really or brown or green or umbrella or pray or grow or rich or drink or pretty or surprise.

Maybe today I won't say anything. Let them guess.

And how come everybody always wants to know my name and address?

One day he told Miss Madison: "I got the mean feeling inside. I guess I want to hit something today."

She brought a big white plastic clown out of the corner. "How about him?" she asked. "Go ahead. Smack him down."

Roger smacked and knocked the white clown down. It bounced right up. He smacked it down again. Once more it bounced up. He hit it hard in the face. It went down and came right back with no change of expression.

"Aw, that's no fun. He doesn't say 'ouch' or get a bwuddy nose or anything."

"These dumb clowns don't know anything," Miss Madison said. "Who was it you were hitting?"

"My fah-thuh," he said. "He nev-vuh waits and listens to me so I can get the wuds out wight. He's always in a big huh-*huh*-wee."

"Well, you fixed him now," she said. "Now he knows how you feel about it."

"Yeah. I wish I could say *rotten*."

"You just did," she said.

"I did?"

"Yup. That was a real good 'rotten' you said there."

"Is that why I got the big eyes?"

"What?"

"When I do something good, you give me the big eyes," he said, pointing his finger above her nose.

She laughed. "I wonder why I do that?"

She wasn't like any of the big people he knew.

"I guess it's because you wike it," he said.

"I guess I do wike it," she said. "I guess I even *like* it." She stuck the tip of her tongue out and pointed at it. "It's okay if I make fun of you sometimes and say it wrong myself. You've got to hear it for yourself. Then you'll be able to say it better."

"It's okay," he said.

"Do you like it when I'm pleased?"

"Yeth," he said.

"Boy, you sure don't get any big eyes on that one! I bet you can say yes-sss."

"Yes-sss," he said. Then, "I got 'em that time."

Miss Madison said, "Let's play a game." She took out a little bag. "Now I'm going to make some wrong sounds and do some wrong things and you have to interrupt me and tell me how to say or do them right. You got that?"

"Uh huh," Roger said.

"Okay, here goes," she said. She took out a small blue plastic spoon. "You see thith thpoon?"

"Yeth," he said.

"Ha!" she said. "I fooled you that time. I said thpoon, not sssspoon. Okay. Now I'm going to fool you again." She took out a white comb. "Now watch. I'm going to part my teeth with my comb."

Roger laughed. "No, no. You pot you heh with a comb."

"Oh, yes, that's right. I part my hair. You got me that time. Now watch this one." She opened a picture book. "Oh, look. Look at this nice picture of the widdle horth."

"It's not a widdle—it's not a *little* horth—no, you got it all wrong. Horsssss! Not horth. And it's not little, it's a big one."

Miss Madison said, "Oops! Excuse me while I put my head in the trash basket," and she went over to the other side of the room and actually did.

"They don't make me do that," Roger said.

"What do you make you do?" she asked, coming back in a dancing happy motion.

"It all depends. When we got company they'd wa-thuh I don't talk at all."

"That's silly," Miss Madison said. "Boy, if that isn't the dopiest thing I ever heard of. I bet if we fixed up those R's they'd let you talk in front of company."

Roger shrugged. "I don't keh."

"I keh," she said.

"Ah we still playing the game?" he asked.

"Nope," she said. "It's time for a little work now." She opened a small box and took out a thin wood object. "Do you know what this is? It's called a depressor." She moved her chair closer to his. "Now here's what we're going to do. It's a good way to help you with that lazy-tongue R sound. We both know you got it so it's no big secret. Right?"

He nodded, his eyes fixed on the little stick.

"Okay, then," she said. "Now you say Lllll. The L sound. When you do I'm going to put this little tongue presser in your mouth and push—"

His eyes were opened wide. "In my mouf?"

"Of course," she said. "It's only a little wooden stick and—"

He shook his head and clamped his mouth shut tightly.

She was looking at him curiously.

"No, no," he said, starting to cry. "Not in mouf. Afwaid. Not in mouf." He struck the stick suddenly out of her hand and sat there rigidly shaking. "Hot! Hot!" he cried and put his hand over his mouth and started to sway back and forth.

Miss Madison closed the little box and got up. She walked across the room and dropped the box of sticks into the basket. Then she came back and stroked his hair.

"I'm so sorry, dear," she said. "Nobody told me your mouth had been burned."

After a while the panic and fright went away and all that remained were the low moaning whimpering sounds that filled the little room with sadness. Miss Madison's eyes weren't the "big ones" now. They were misty and her gentle face reflected in its concern the agony in his.

"It's all right, sweetheart," she said and drew him closer to her side. The softness of the smooth golden-skinned arms enfolding him and the warmth of her body began to comfort. He clung to her fiercely now as he moaned and trembled, her soft soothing words easing away his terror.

"It probably happened a long long time ago when you were a very little boy," she said. "But it's all over now. Cry it away, dear."

It was a styptic pencil.

He was three years old when he found it on his father's dresser. It was in a little glass tube with a cap on the end. It was nice and white with a piece of red colored wrapping and it looked very interesting, like sugar or candy.

Tiny fingers snatched it off the dresser, got the cap off and the little hard sugar thing out. One end was blunt and had no paper covering, so that looked like the right end to start with.

The piece of paper was easy for his fingers. It uncurled and fell right off. The white sugar thing in his mouth seemed just right for sucking. Maybe it was some new kind of lollipop.

He sat on the floor near the big bed wondering when the good sweet taste was going to come, chortling happily, his head thrown back against the coverlet.

He couldn't believe it when the pain started.

Suddenly, outrageously, his mouth and tongue were burning with a terrible hurt. A fire was inside there, in his mouth, all the way through, and now his tongue was burning as if there was a hole inside it. He tried to scream but couldn't get the white thing that was not candy or sugar out of his moaning mouth.

His parents, downstairs sitting around the pool with friends, finally heard him screaming. They found him writhing on the floor, banging his head to get rid of the pain.

Before they took him to the doctor the mother grabbed his hands away from his mouth and slapped them hard.

"Bad boy, bad boy!" she said in the angry voice. "Don't you ever do that again!" His eyes, already swollen in agony, could hardly see the big white face and the mad mouth.

The father didn't hug him either, but stooped down to pick up some of the crushed white pieces on the floor, wipe them off and put them back in the little glass tube. Then he looked around for the screw cap that went on it.

"When are you going to teach this kid not to put everything he sees in his greedy little mouth," he told the mother. "I better find that cap now before somebody cuts his foot on it."

"It's all right now. It's all right, little boy," Miss Madison was crooning to him in a soft kind of sing-song voice. He tried to bury his head deeper into her side, into her warmth, wanting to hold on to this nice feeling of being loved if only for a little while.

CHAPTER SEVEN

SHE WAS in the large room near the window, painting. She didn't like having her "painting mood" disturbed but he'd been thinking a lot about the increasing number of visitors lately and being left alone in the New York City apartment with the wind rattling windows at night while she went out to dinner or to the theater or just out *period*.

"Do you think you'll get m-mm- meh-meh . . . find anoth-a husband?"

Even the word *married* had to have an R in it.

The mother's eyes rolled dramatically and the thin lower lip exhaled a noticeable sigh. "Roger, how many times have I asked you not to talk to me when I'm painting!"

See, I told you. She never forgets.

"I fo-got. Okay. So will you?"

"I suppose you want another father," she said.

"Well, not exactly. It's just—I just—well—"

"Not that you really ever had one in the first place. Any more than I really had a husband," she added sourly.

"Oh, Pop was okay," he said.

"He was? Really? Was he? Tell me how," she said. "Perhaps I missed something along the way."

The boy thought for a while but nothing came to mind that would change the cold stare with which she mocked him. Finally, he said: "Well—he nev—he nev —he didn't hit me."

"Now isn't that sad," she said. "That's real sad. 'He didn't hit me.' I suppose you're implying that I have."

The boy shrugged his shoulders.

"Don't forget he hardly ever saw you," the mother said, "hardly spent a minute with you. I'm the one that was stuck with you. Well, don't look so surprised; it's true, isn't it? I had you on my hands all the time. Morning, noon, and night. And you were quite a hateful child, Roger, if you don't mind my saying so. Very. As obstinate as a mule." She tossed her hair and sniffed. "Well, naturally, I lost my patience at times. You've got to admit you're a very stubborn child, Roger."

I suppose so, he thought.

She was looking fretfully at the large canvas with its low-keyed muddy colors in splotches, brightened by some discordant yellow-greens.

"Now you've spoiled my mood. How do you expect me to paint with all your silly questions? When I find a new husband, I'll let you know," she said sarcastically. "But I'll tell you one thing—the next one's going to be a *man*. All man," she added viciously jabbing her brush into some pigment for another one of the big muddy splotches.

What is that crack supposed to mean? he thought. *I remember he had hair on his chest.*

Though the body was sort of mushy and flabby, he remembered, *and there weren't many muscles.*

"Besides, it's none of your business anyway," she said. "If I feel like getting married, I'll get married. Now is there anything else you'd like to know?"

"Yeah. When ah you going to finish that stupid painting?" he said, starting out of the room, not listening to the names she was calling him. He grabbed his coat and yelled: "I'm going out."

"Where?"

"Just out," he was at the door now. "Maybe you'll be lucky and I'll fall under a taxicab." The door slammed behind him louder than he intended.

He jabbed his finger at the elevator button and kept it there until the one near it glowed red and he knew somebody woke up at last downstairs. He jabbed the button again. "That's for taking so long," he said.

The other elevator, going down, got there first.

He hoped the operator wasn't in a talkative mood. *I'll pretend I got an earache.* The trouble with the lisp that sneaked in and the R's that came out W's, was that the more you said, the more you exposed yourself. It was like once you had a speech defect you'd lost your membership card in the human race.

He thought bitterly, nobody could understand a word dolphins said and yet all the big brains went around bragging about what great communicators these dolphins were. Only who wants to be a dolphin?

To keep from sounding like a baby, you kept most of your thoughts to yourself. You answered only what you had to. If you couldn't think of a substitute for a word with an R in it, sometimes it was easier to pretend you were deaf.

Sorry, Jack, I'm deaf so I can't hear you. So I can't answer you, naturally.

Sometimes it was easier to pretend you didn't know.

Who? Paul Revere? Never heard of him. Only you didn't say that because it had the Jonah words, the ones with the R's. Instead you said something like: "Who? Him? Uh-uh. I dunno." Or you could shake your head and make out you were really dumb. That was the whole trouble. To keep from sounding like a fool you ended up a moron, for God's sake.

Sometimes he spoke out of sheer defiance. Nobody owned the world and if he wanted to say the words his way that was his business. The heck with them.

Sometimes he did it to test a person. When he spoke to the girl in the red swirling skirt it was because he hated to be accepted on false pretenses. It was better sometimes to let them know what you really sounded like so they didn't drop you like a hot potato later.

That usually came after the look, of course.

The look went two ways. Sometimes the look went the other way; that is, away from you, as if they couldn't stand hearing you.

The second way was the one that looked you right in the eye and said: *Are you for real? Are you kidding*

*with that baby talk? Excuse me but I got no time to
play in your sandbox. Go back to kindergarten!*

It turned out to be one of his better elevator rides.
For one thing, the operator didn't feel like talking.
Old George just stood there with his hand on the
lever control, his jaw all swollen solid, looking as if he
wanted to cry: "Honest, my jaw ain't always swollen.
It's only because I got this rotten toothache from this
impacted wisdom tooth. You wait and see. Tomorrow
I'll be beautiful. I'll have a jaw like real people.
Honest. Don't look now, huh?"

That was only part of his good luck. The best part
was seeing the tall slim girl leaning languidly there.
The girl from PH, upstairs. One of the elevator men
had mentioned her name. It was Pat Bentley. A name
he could say.

Her lips parted in a genuinely delighted expression.
"Well, hi, Baxter," she said. "How's it going?"

"Fine," he said.

How come she's so glad to see me?

He wished now that he had answered, "Hi, Miss
Bentley." Then she would have known that he knew
who she was. It was too late to do anything about it
now. *Dope,* he told himself. He'd seen her picture in
many different magazines since their first meeting in
the elevator. He had cut some of them out before his
mother made a big scene about it.

Somehow Miss Bentley didn't photograph as skinny.

Sometimes she would be sitting, looking bored, on
a windy sandswept dune, wearing the new styles in

sweaters that were too big for her, over a bathing suit. Sometimes she would be on the deck of a sailboat, leaning easily against some rope, wearing Bermuda shorts or different kinds of sailor outfits for girls. The wind would be ruffling her hair, blowing it all over her face. But she would be looking way off into the distance, miles away, like that was the only thing that mattered.

Now she was wearing something black and slinky, so tight he wondered how she could even walk in it, and around her shoulders a fur wrap. *Sure not much for this cold weather*, he thought. There was a big man beside her and she was holding his arm. *She must be going out on a date*, he guessed.

The man looked a lot older and like a fighter. His neck was thick, and on it he carried his head stiff and straight as if they were all one piece. His shoulders were thick, too, and very wide. His chest was deep, held high. His hair was mostly gray, his eyes were large and black, and he had a lot of deep lines creasing his craggy face. Dressed all in black and carrying a black evening hat, everything about him was neat and clean and in place. He even smelled nice. For some strange reason, Roger felt glad the tall girl was going out on a date with this man.

They were at the lobby now and the doors swished open. Before he could stop himself Roger said: "Have a good time."

The black-fringed violet eyes rewarded him.

"Thanks, doll," she said, and swept gracefully out of the car.

Roger waited for the big man to follow. He tilted

his head stiffly instead, leaning forward in a slight bow, smiling.

"*Après vous*," he said, the outstretched open big hand indicating that Roger was first. He hesitated a second then walked out.

The doorman was wearing earmuffs, his face red. He spun the door. The girl stepped through. Roger tried to hang back, but felt the big man's hand on his shoulder, and strong fingers tapping him twice.

"No, no. You first."

The soft voice sounded like a French actor's, a big blond blue-eyed man with wide sloping shoulders and carelessly worn hair whom Roger had seen in the movies.

Tom, the doorman, said cheerily: "Yes, sir. Good evening, sir. How are you this evening, sir?"

"Fine," Roger said, then had to step fast to get out before the doors spun him around again inside. That was all he needed, he thought. The big man checked the speed of the doors with his hand and followed Roger through.

"Good night, sir," the doorman called after him, opening the outside single glass door.

An icy blast of wind pushed Roger back against the security of the building wall. A taxicab was waiting at the curb, near the building canopy, and the doorman already had its door open. The tall girl folded herself up inside. The big man was about to follow when suddenly she leaned out.

"Can we drop you any place, Baxter?" incredibly she asked him.

Huh? he said to himself.

Wake up, you dummy, she's talking to you.

"Gee, no thanks," he called back, fighting the wind, "I wasn't going any place," so surprised and pleased he could hardly speak the words.

"Oh, come on," she said. "That's what taxicabs are for."

The man was looking at him, waiting in the wind that blew his hair and whipped his coat and trousers. Roger's mind reeled. He took a step forward, resisting the wind, bending forward.

"W-which way you going?"

"Thataway," she said and flung out her arm in a sweeping exaggerated gesture that embraced everywhere.

Come on! You want her to think you're a dope, too?

"Okay," he said. "H-how about Times S-Skweh?" He had never been there but had heard and read of it.

"It's a deal," she yelled. "Hop in."

He looked up at the big man and the man nodded and smiled. "It is all right," he said, reading Roger's mind. Roger started into the cab and once again hesitated, not sure of where to sit.

The pale face was framed in black at the far window. She patted the space next to her. "Park it right here, doll," she said.

Roger slid in, the big man behind him. The doorman slammed the door.

"Good night, Miss Bentley," he said and retreated inside the big building.

"You heard the man," she told the driver. "Times Square, first stop."

The car made a wide sweeping U-turn in the wide street. It was Roger's first time in a New York City taxi. The meter box over the dashboard up front already indicated thirty cents. There was a picture of the driver in a thin black frame on the back of the seat directly ahead of Roger. He read the man's name: Lenny Gordon, and his hack license number. The heat blowing from the heater in front had a faint smell of alcohol and despite the cold night, the cab was fairly warm. The driver hit his brakes for a red light at West End Avenue, and turned right when it flashed green. In California, Roger remembered, you could make a right turn on a red. *It's different here; everything is different,* he thought.

The tall girl was kicking his leg. "It's a good thing you woke up," she said. "I was beginning to think I wasn't a good kicker any more."

Roger grinned. Whatever she said came out just right.

"Okay, doll," she said. "Tell me about yourself. I don't know a thing except you came from—what's that wild place again? Oh, yes. California. LA, maybe?"

He nodded. Then after a few seconds he said, surprised himself to hear the words, "I don't talk much. You see I got this speech defect."

"I don't hear any," she said.

"I can't say any wuds with ah's in them," he said.

The man on his right leaned forward slightly, addressing his question to the tall beautiful girl.

"*Qu'est-ce que c'est?*" he asked.

"His R's, Roger," she said. "He says he can't pro-nounce the words with R's in them."

"Oh?" said the man. "That is too bad. *Pourquoi?*"

"I don't know."

Roger? Did she call the man Roger?

"Is that name—what she called you—"

The big man put his gloved hand in a mock formal way on his chest and bowed slightly in a rocking motion.

"Roger Tunnell," he said, stressing the last syllables.

"That's my name, too," Roger said, marveling.

"No kidding?" the girl said. "Baxter, you mean to tell me you're a Roger, too?"

"Yeh," he said.

"No wonder I love you," she said in her kidding way.

"Only it's anoth-a wud I can't say," he said. "You know. Because of—" He stopped. *Was he talking too much?*

"You can do it," said the burly big man. "You can say your R's. You must work at it. Practice. More and more. You can do it." He said "it" so it sounded "eet."

Roger shrugged. He liked the man so he didn't mind the lecture. "It's not so easy," he said.

The tall girl touched his arm. "Whatever he says, Baxter, you can believe. He was paralyzed once and couldn't talk for six years. He *made* himself talk."

"No kidding?" *How could he do that*, he wondered.

"I once had a bullet right here," the man said in his low voice. He opened his muffler and put a finger near his windpipe. "A present from the Nazis during the war. You cannot see the scar in this light but it is there."

"And you couldn't talk—all that time?"

"The voice box, it was paralyzed."

"So how did you do it?"

"It was not easy either," the man said. "Not only not to be able to talk. Not to make any sound at all. Not even to make the sound or cry of an animal. Not even to hear myself moan in my misery."

He was silent for a while and Roger, watching his face as the flickering passing street lights lit it, knew he was far away, trying to moan away a hurt.

"But, when they told me it was hopeless, that I would never talk again, then I knew I would have to work out a way for myself. I knew some day I would meet some wonderful person like this Miss Bentley. And I knew when I did, I would want to talk to her."

"Oh," said Roger, pleased with the thought.

He wondered how many nights in the six years the big man had cried silently in the night.

"That is why I said you can do it, my young friend. You can make yourself do anything."

"Roger was with the French underground," the tall girl said. "After the Nazis caught up with him and shot him, they left him there to die. Only he didn't do what he was supposed to, then, either."

I wonder if I could keep myself from dying. How could you do that?

The Frenchman pointed to his head. "Up here. Here is where the control is. Here is where the orders come from. The brain tells the body what to do. So you tell yourself: Look here! This is what I want to do. No argument. No excuses. Just let us do it, please. And right away. Now!"

"Sounds like a good idea," said the boy. "Maybe I'll twy it myself some day."

The cabbie was hitting the brakes and brushing the curb. Roger heard honking and shrill whistles. Dazzling lights were all around him. He had never seen so many people on a city street.

"Timesquare," the driver said. "Whicht corner ya wan' Mac? Nort aw Souf?"

"I bet you're from Brooklyn," the tall girl said.

"What else?" said the driver.

That night Roger didn't sleep in his bed.

He was in a cave deep in the mountains of France, in the Alps or anyway somewhere near. He wasn't quite sure where the Alps were, exactly, but he could see himself and everything clearly. . . .

The inside of the cave was shaped like a giant armadillo, hollowed out of stone. The entrance was low and narrow, extending to the swollen belly and back, where he could stand, then narrowing itself down again.

He himself was older, grown surprisingly big, with thick shoulders and a wide chest. His neck looked pretty strong, too; his face tanned and as tough probably as leather, lined now with great lines of weariness, sunken and hollow about the cheekbones. He had not eaten for a long time, probably not for days.

On a small table inside the cave was a lantern. No, candles. Their flickering and sputtering threw uneven waves of light on the rough maps on the table. There was a radio transmitter behind the table on a small shelf cut out of the rock, silent now. But he was expecting a vital message at any second.

Snow was falling outside the cave and it was bitter cold, so cold that he had to warm his big hands on the candles instead of the lantern which could have been better for that. There was a long blacknosed rifle leaning against the cave wall. There was a thin sharp knife, probably a dagger, on the table. There was a sword, too, a long, sharp —well, maybe he didn't need the sword. Forget the sword.

His mind erased the sword.

He knew the Nazis were even now hunting for him, the Gray Ghost, but that vital radio message very well could be an order to sabotage another troop train. Or perhaps cover a secret paratroop drop and then hide the men until it was safe for them to carry out their mission.

He watched the snow falling, saw the drifts form, knowing that his only hope now was the deep new snow to cover his footsteps. How could you walk in fallen snow without leaving tracks? Of course an avalanche could wipe them out, too, but he couldn't depend on that. His father had never instructed him in walking in snow without leaving tracks. He hoped when his side, the Underground, caught up with his father he wouldn't have to tell them the truth, that he had abandoned his post and run away.

He worked alone now. It was better that way. And how he was feared; this silent strong man— who yet had the words of command ready if needed, there was no question about that—and the strength of many men in his fingers. How many had he killed so far? Perhaps twenty. How many trains derailed with his uncanny skill at setting the timer against the demo charges? How many bridges demolished and the rumbling monster tanks?

The Nazis would be surprised to learn that Group 5, his code name, was but a single man. A man who had the strength of five. Was that too much? he wondered.

The interior of the cave measured about twenty feet deep, the mouth opening just wide enough for slipping through, and the supplies were hidden along the walls in the rear: the TNT boxes, the wires needed in his work, the pliers to cut them with.

It was difficult having to lug the heavy boxes of ammo over the mountains to this secret hideout. Perhaps that was why he was so tired now. That could be it all right. There were several boxes of fuses, and others with cartridges, the spare ammo, perhaps some grenades.

He had to stamp his feet to stay awake. How many nights had he gone now without sleep? Three? Perhaps four. That was possible. He had gone four nights without sleep. Maybe that was why he was so tired, come to think of it. But after tonight's mission he would be able to rest a few hours. A leader of the secret resistance forces— one of the dreaded Maquis—was that it?—had little time for sleep. That would come later when France was free again.

Even though he was so very sleepy and tired, his senses were cat-acute. A Gray Ghost had that faculty. Now he heard a soft muffled sound outside the cave. Hardly anyone else could have identified that sound as a footstep. A footstep in the snow. A careful footstep. He bent his head forward swiftly and blew out the candles, reached for his rifle, found it at once in the dark. It paid to be efficient.

The worn-smooth cold stock of the rifle comforted his hands. Then he remembered the knife, the long thin dagger. He found that too in the darkness, without even rustling the paper maps, and slipped it inside his belt. Perhaps his boot might be better, he thought, just in case he got captured. He removed the knife from his belt and put it inside his boot. His feet were very cold.

If it happened to be a Nazi search party, he was cornered all right.

It was too dark outside to see anything. There had been a moon but it had gone behind some cloud. He waited inside that cold dark cave, holding his breath, having automatically slid to his stomach to present less of a target. He felt the chill of the ground. He wondered what the temperature was. Probably ten below at least.

Then suddenly there was a light shining in his eyes. He felt the heat on his eyelids. He jerked his rifle into position and pulled the trigger—only nothing happened. Was it jammed? He made a mental note to carry grenades next time. You had to be prepared for anything!

Well, he would have to charge, that was all there was to it. He got to his knees and roared like an angry lion but found he couldn't move. Hands were holding him down. Who could hold Group 5? He shook his head in disbelief. Perhaps he had been drugged or something. That was most likely the reason. Drugs could do that to you. Weaken your whole system, inside and out.

Then came the sneering voice of the Nazi patrol leader who had tricked him somehow, only the voice sounded like his mother's.

"Roger, wake up, wake up."

He felt a stinging smart on his face. He must have scraped his face on a rock or something on the ground there. He blinked as the attacker shook him and then he was awake and there She was, all right, standing over him, looking mean-eyed. What had he done this time?

"For God's sake! Do you want to wake up the whole house? The neighbors will think I'm killing you."

"I guess I was having a dweam," he said, suddenly feeling foolish and deflated.

"A dream?" She repeated sarcastically. "Some dream. That wasn't a dream, it was a nightmare."

Now he would never know the ending, he thought bitterly. Did he fight his way out of it, fight out of trouble again, slip away like the Gray Ghost could? he wondered. Or was this the time they captured him, put the bullet in his neck and left him lying there to die in the snow, outside the cave shaped so much like an armadillo hollowed out.

He tried to visualize himself crawling over the snowy mountains trailing blood, refusing to die. But then, he couldn't leave, could he? He still had that vital radio message to receive.

Finally he had to admit it was impossible to know the real ending. He leaned down over the side of the bed and picked up the blankets.

No wonder it was so cold in that cave, you dope, he told himself. *You kicked off all your blankets.*

CHAPTER EIGHT

MORNINGS were the worst.

Mornings meant getting up and making his own breakfast.

Mornings meant waking Her to get his daily allowance, money for the bus fare to school and back, money for the school cafeteria hot lunch.

"Hello. You up?"

Mornings meant getting a look of contempt right off the bat.

"Of course I'm up. You woke me so I'm up."

"Okay. So I need money."

"All right. How much do you need?"

As if She didn't know. They'd only gone over it about a hundred times so far.

"Thirty cents for bus fare? That's outrageous for a school kid. You ought to get a discount."

Yeah, I'll tell 'em. They'll give me a special discount. Because my ears match.

"And lunch. I need lunch money, too."

"Where do they get off charging fifty cents for hamburgers? Are you sure you're buying a hamburger with that money?"

No, I'm getting a steak. With champagne.

She could have given him the money the night before. But the night before She was always too busy to discuss it or too nervous going out or expecting company.

"We'll talk about it later," She would say, moving away from him. It was as if he had just asked for the family jewels or a quarter of a million dollars or permission to rob a bank. And "later" never came.

Sometimes he would walk home to save the fifteen cents. The other kids usually headed for the Pizza Parlor or a hamburger hangout but he couldn't do much with fifteen cents there. Then they headed for the Broadway record shops, throwing money around like water, feeling no guilt or pain. Busby was an expensive private school. If you didn't have money you sent your kids to the public schools.

He knew his father made a lot of money.

So how come She always acts like we're poor?

The other kids got double and three times what he did a week, some even more. He didn't care about that so much. What he envied was their getting it all at one time, in advance, so they could decide for themselves how to spend it, how to live and get through the week with it.

Without having to wake up somebody every single morning to fight about the stinking one dollar he needed.

He had enough trouble every morning worrying
about how he was going to get along with Mr. Rawling without worrying about the money.

He knew his father sent Her a check every week but
he didn't know the amount. From the broken-marriage
kids in Los Angeles he knew that usually large
amounts were given when the parties broke up. It was
like some kind of code out there.

I'm pretty sure he's sending us plenty. Maybe She's
afraid I'll spread the news and get kidnapped for a big
ransom. Yeah, I'll bet. She wouldn't buy me back for
fifty cents.

He wondered how much She would ever buy him
back for, if She really had to. Five dollars maybe?
Ten? A hundred?

Hey, are you kidding? A hundred dollars for you?
How's about fifteen cents?

Well, I don't know for sure.

Well, do you know anything for sure?

Yeah, I'm sick and tired of the whole thing. Why'd
they have to break up anyway?

They stood it for fifteen years; they could have
stood it a little longer.

Well, how much longer would you say? he asked
himself.

I don't know exactly. A couple of more years maybe,
anyway.

You think that would have made such a big dif-
ference?

Well, I don't know. But it would have helped
with right now. Right now is what I'm talking about.

Look, do me a favor, will you? Go cry on somebody else's shoulder.

For the first time that he could remember, he found himself wondering about the age of his parents and if that had anything to do with it. When they were interviewed the first time he went to a speech clinic, he remembered his mother made a big stink about it when they got home.

"What business is it of theirs how old I am?" She had raged, slamming the door shut to keep him out of it.

"I hope you didn't tell them the truth," the father said next. "You should have taken the Fifth."

"Well, it just so happens that I did. And she gave me a look as if I was queer or something. Then she wanted to know why we waited so long to have a child. Can you tell me what the hell business that is of theirs?"

"How should I know?" he heard the father say. "Maybe they need a case history so they know what's wrong."

"Just because the kid can't say his lousy R's they make a big federal case out of it. You know what else she asked me? 'How old was the boy when you first noticed it? What happened that day, that week, that month'?"

"What do you mean what happened that day, that week, that month?"

"Out of the ordinary. How about that? How about *that?* Can you remember way back then? How old he was? And what week? What are we supposed to do, keep a record?"

"Well, what did you tell them?"

"Who could remember that far back? I said two years."

"It wasn't two years. He could hardly talk at all at two. It was five years."

"It wasn't five years. It was long before five."

"Wait—I think it was four years."

"Four?" she had said. "Well maybe. Anyway, what happened? Do you remember anything that happened to do it to him?"

"Sure," the father had said. "Wasn't that the time you locked him in his room because he wouldn't ask for his own hamburger in that restaurant?"

"He wasn't five then. He was six. And it wasn't a restaurant. It was that lousy college. That UCLA."

It's a good thing I remember, he told himself. *It's a good thing somebody remembers.*

He remembered it vividly still. One of his bad times.

They were sitting at a white table that felt like marble in a big bright room filled with older, bigger people. It was on a Saturday and somebody else sat with them. A man. But not his father.

He was tall and thin with a very tan face and short hair, and he wore dark green sunglasses, a floppy dark blue shirt, white rumpled pants, white socks and white sneakers.

He was a writer, always laughing and kidding, an old school friend of his mother's. He had visited their house that day. His mother wanted to see an art exhibit at the college and they went down in her car. It was a nice sunny California day.

Where was his father? Working, as always.

He was six years old and after She parked the car it was a long walk. After a while his feet began to burn from the hot pavement and it was hard to keep up with the long striding man and Her. She seemed in a pretty happy mood. The man saw him limping along and suggested cutting the walk short and going back for the car.

"No, Victor. He does this deliberately. Now, Roger, you wanted to come along, so keep up. Keep up. I'm warning you."

Up hundreds of brick steps, so wide they could have held a parade, and when you got to the top you could see all of Westwood and Brentwood and Bel-Air, the white houses all tucked in their own places in the mountains. Then along walks laced with green and bordered in brilliant colors, flowers and cactus in the corners of buildings. All the buildings seemed to be red brick with high arches over big doors and all the steps leading into them very wide. It was a warm Saturday afternoon with just enough students around to remind you it was a college in case you forgot.

The art exhibit was in a low long modern-looking building with a lady sitting inside at a desk selling small catalogs, for which the man gave some money.

The paintings were all pretty big, something like the kind his mother did all the time. He liked

the colors. There were a lot of happy-looking
paintings there. He moved around the room
quickly and was waiting outside for them when
they finished, looking at a big gold metal statue
made of a lot of different shapes like an airplane
engine that probably fell apart and was stuck together again. It didn't fit right anymore but he
liked it better this way. He wanted to stick his
head inside and look up at the sky through all
the holes in it but he was a little afraid of it.

His mother made some joke about him being an
art critic and then they walked downhill along
curving paths and there were students sprawled
out all around on the grass or on benches, reading books. A big bell somewhere chimed the
hour, three very loud bongs that vibrated and
hung in the air for about ten steps.

Then they came to a different kind of building,
high and white and looking something like a ship,
with colored umbrellas outside and small tables
and slatted redwood benches along the white
walls. The man with the sunglasses told them this
student building was open to the public on Sat-
urdays.

There was a room full of food machines inside
the first room. His mother asked him if he was
hungry yet and he had been hungry for a long
time so now he said yes.

She put some coins in for a thick sandwich
wrapped in wax paper and a small container of
milk. The man found some straws for him.

He sat at a large round whitetopped table that

felt cool in a very large cheerful room. There were gigantic pictures on the walls; pictures of football players crashing into each other, some with black stuff like ink on their faces, and pictures of cheerleaders leaping off the ground with their arms stretched out, some looking pleased, some angry and a few surprised. He heard music and saw the big console where the records dropped down and clicked into place and started to play. The music sounded good in that big room and he liked being there, sitting at a table in the same room with all the big kids.

There was a book case, the biggest he had ever seen, halfway to the high ceiling, from one side of the big room to the other, separated in the center for people to come through carrying food on brown trays.

His mother finally helped him get the sandwich open. One of the tiny metal staples holding the wax paper corners together stuck Her finger and She got very angry.

Then the tall man came back with a brown tray, too, on which were two hamburgers and small cardboard baskets filled with long brown french fried potatoes. They smelled good. He wished he had waited another couple of minutes and gotten the hamburger with the french fries.

His own sandwich was roast beef, with soggy white bread and tired looking lettuce. He started to pick out the wilted lettuce and She gave him a dirty look. Then he tried picking out some of the fat and a piece of string that happened to be stuck in his meat, and She didn't like that either.

Finally when he tried eating it he found that he didn't like it. He looked at the hamburgers and the little baskets of french fries and wished someone had told him about them before. The man must have noticed, and asked if he wanted a hamburger. He started to say yea, he even *looked* "yes," but he heard Her voice.

"Now don't spoil him, Victor. He already has a sandwich." She spread apart the wax paper and saw the lettuce he had picked out and the string and the fat. "Why aren't you eating your sandwich, Roger?" She demanded.

He just told her he wasn't hungry anymore and put the plastic straw into the milk container. Two bites of the soggy sandwich was all he could manage; the bread stuck to the roof of his mouth and he was afraid he would choke.

"That sandwich cost forty cents. You wanted it so you eat it."

He shook his head, beginning to get a little frightened.

She pushed it closer to him. "Go on, eat it."

He said he wasn't hungry now and did he have to? There were some college kids at the table nearest them, big boys and laughing blond-haired pretty girls. For some reason he began to feel very nervous.

"So it's forty cents," the man called Victor said. "Let me get the kid a hamburger, Con."

She made a twitching grimace with her

mouth and turned to face him again. "Would you like a hamburger, Roger?"

Before he could stop himself, his dumb head was nodding and he said, "Yes."

He didn't like the expression in her eyes. She opened her bag and took a bill out of her wallet. "Here's a dollar," she said. "Now you go up there and get one for yourself. And one for me."

His eyes shifted from the dollar bill to where her head indicated "up there" was. He saw a long glass counter and showcase with some cakes in it, shining silvery aluminum poles set in the white floor with some kind of tape or rope on them strung out to other poles. He wondered what that was for.

Then he saw the big people standing in line. They belonged there and he didn't, he knew. They were standing in two lines, one starting at the left side, coming to the counter, and curving to the right. The line on the right side worked the same way, only curving to the left. Ladies in blue uniforms behind the glass counter kept moving to a big opening at the back to yell, reach in, and come back with hamburgers or pizza. They handed them to the big kids, got money and rang a cash register.

He knew if he went up there his head couldn't come halfway up the glass counter and none of the busy women in blue would see him. To ask for the little baskets of french fries, which he wanted the most, would mean using words he couldn't say right any more, not since his mouth and tongue got hurt that time when he was three.

The big college kids would look down at him and laugh, the ladies in blue pretend they couldn't see him there and for him to stand up, please.

No hamburger or french fries were worth all this, he knew even then. He started to shake his head No, but the dollar bill came closer and he could see the blurred picture and writing and numbers on it before he pushed it away.

Her voice was flat and mean now.

"You said you wanted a hamburger. Now take this money and go up and get it."

He shook his head again, unable to talk now, leaning away from Her in the big chair until he could feel it hard on his back, his body stiff and taut, his legs beginning to tremble.

"Oh, come on, Connie. I'll get it for him. The kid's embarrassed about going up there."

The man got up from the table but She put her hand on his arm and he sat down again.

She flashed Roger a look of fury. "No, Victor. Please don't interfere. He's got to learn to do things he doesn't like." How could She have such a pretty face and still be so mean? the boy wondered. "Now, Roger, there's nothing to be afraid of. You just step up there and ask for your hamburger. Here's the money."

She reached for his hand to put the bill inside it but he clenched it tightly shut and She couldn't get it open.

"Do you want a hamburger or not?" She was saying, her voice too loud now with the music suddenly stopped.

Through his tears he could see the big kids at the next table watching. He was crying now when he didn't want to. Not in front of Victor. Not in front of the college kids, the nice big boys and girls. He'd have given a million dollars not to cry then. Now Her voice changed and She gave him a different look. This look pretended to be friendly.

"Do you want mother to get it for you?"

He couldn't say yes now. He knew She was out to trap him. Twist what he said and make it come out just the way She wanted. He shook his head No again. She didn't like that. She waved the dollar bill in his face.

"Go buy yourself a hamburger."

Mutely, he shook his head.

"I thought you said you were hungry. Here. Take the money and go up there. They won't eat you."

He was shuddering and shaking now, hating Her with every twitching fibre, afraid of Her, hating Her. Hating Her.

The man tried to help. "For God's sake, Connie, let go, will you? He says he doesn't want it."

She gave him an exasperated annoyed look. "Please, Victor. You don't know this boy. He likes to make scenes like this. He does it all the time to humiliate me."

The man shook his head helplessly as if he
didn't understand. He looked at her, not laughing or kidding now about anything, and pushed
his plate away. Then he pushed his chair back
and stood up. "Let's get out of here," he said in
a thick voice.

"No," She said. "He's got to learn. Now,
Roger, I'm telling you for the last time—"

The man interrupted Her, with now a growling
threatening note in his voice. "Knock it off,
Connie. You're not only scaring hell out of the
kid, you're scaring me, too. Let's go. Come on!"

She jerked the dollar bill back and put it inside Her wallet with a snap. Then She closed
the zipper of Her big bag with a vicious tug.
There wasn't any expression at all now in Her
large staring eyes. This was even more frighten-
ing to Roger than when She just looked mad.
This was Her we'll-take-care-of-this-later look.

"All right, Roger," She said, getting up, a wry
smile on Her lips. "Have it your own way."

He twisted himself off the chair as if it were
burning him and started for the door.

He didn't want to bother now thinking about
what came later. You didn't want to remember
everything, for Pete's sake.

CHAPTER NINE

THE ACID TONGUE of Mr. Rawling framed the sentence in his soft sly scathing way.

"I believe the book is called *The Rubaiyat of Omar Khayyam*, Roger," he said. "Hasn't our Miss Clemm done anything for you yet?"

Well, as a matter of fact she has, Roger answered silently. *But I guess it's really going to be up to me.*

The sign said SPEECH CLINIC. Black letters on a white card in a thin black frame, placed exactly in the center of the top half of a door stained the color of walnut although it could have been the natural wood itself. *Well, what's the difference anyway? It's only a door. It's no big deal if it's phoney or real. The point is I have to go through it. That's the important thing right now.*

Was he supposed to knock? he wondered, gripping the glossy hard knob. Well, that didn't matter much any more, either. He'd find out about it soon enough, as usual.

The door opened easily and without squeaks. When he shut it, there wasn't any slam because of the brass air-pressure braking cylinder on top. It closed with a nice soft snick. Under perfect control.

He had to admit it. He respected that door.

The room was large and carpeted a dark red, like burgundy, he thought, like old wine. The walls were natural wood rubbed to a soft glowing patina. The light on the desk was low and not glaring, the desk itself large enough to hold all its papers without looking cluttered. There was a big green leather chair near it.

Well, one good thing, it doesn't look like a hospital anyway.

No glaring white walls or the black-and-white vinyl floor or the smell that told you the people in charge hated bugs and were afraid of them. Even more important, he realized, was the feeling of quiet he got from the room.

Hey, it looks as if I'm the only patient here! He liked that too. Not a single other sufferer around.

All right, Miss Clemm; don't worry. I'm noticing you too. I wish everybody luck here and that's no lie.

Now, he told himself, *please do me a favor and don't fink out here. And stop looking around for that dumb two-way mirror. If they got one, that's their business.*

What do you mean it's their business? Isn't it our business, too?

Oh, for cryin' out loud, grow up, will you? If they

got doctors watching, it's to help, isn't it? And that's what you're here for, isn't it? For help? I mean, you've got this problem and you haven't done such a hot job handling it yourself, if you notice, right? So do me a favor and don't get in the way here. Just butt out.

He made himself walk over to her desk. The framed diplomas on the wall behind her informed anybody who cared to know that Roberta Clemm had achieved a master's degree and a doctorate in speech pathology at the University of Edinburgh.

Okay, that's fine. I'm glad you're such an expert because we're going to need all the help we can get. So let's go already and get this meeting started.

She was busy with a tape recorder, taking notes and listening to sounds he could not hear. She didn't take the least notice that he was in the room and he was glad of that. It gave him a chance to study her.

Roberta Clemm sat square and stocky. He wasn't prepared for such a massive woman, bigger and wider than any he had ever seen and twice as ugly. A thick unruly mop of dark yellow hair cascaded over the top of her broad face. Her eyes were small and slanted downward giving her a sad look. Her nose was blunt and flat and her great outthrust jaw jutted like a bulldog's, giving her wide firm mouth a grimace.

She was frowning now as she concentrated on her tapes, and screwing up her mouth in a grinning double arc. Under a loose black sweater was a light yellow blouse, open at the throat. Her hands were busy, writing quickly on the file cards she held; strong shapely hands, the fingers long and square-tipped. She wore a brown skirt and he had the feeling her shoes would be plain oxfords with low comfortable heels.

As he moved closer he heard the sound coming from the spinning tapes of the recorder—a high-pitched childish treble of a voice, and although he heard it distinctly he couldn't understand a word being said.

Miss Clemm saw him now and gave him a huge exaggerated wink. She beckoned him closer. He took another step and listened hard. It was a girl's voice, he was sure of that. But that was all he was sure of. Then the odd cadence registered with him and he remembered the old nursery rhyme he was hearing:

> "Tippo Tymuh meh a pyemuh
>   Doh to peh,
> Ted Tippo Tyemuh to duh pyemuh,
>   Yeh meh tee ooh weh!"

Boy, that's real baby talk. That's even worse than me. That little girl's got trouble.

The speech therapist's finger was on the stop button and the whirling tapes whistled to a halt. She screwed up her lips and wrote furiously on a white file card. Then her eyes lifted to Roger's.

"Can you guess how old that girl is?"

"Oh," he said, taken back, "I guess about five—maybe six."

"Hmph," she snorted. "Sixteen would be a better guess."

No kidding! Hey, that's pretty bad for sixteen. Well, so anyway, I was right in a way. That case is in trouble and needs help.

"See what kind of a detective you are on this one," she was saying. Her finger jabbed the start button, the tapes started, and Roger heard another voice. This one sounded like a little boy. He was sure of that. And, after a while, he recognized this old nursery rhyme too:

> "Tinko, tinko, itto tah,
> Ow I wondah eh ooh ah
> Up puh buh duh woh so high
> Yike a dye min en duh kye."

She switched it off and looked at Roger with a quizzical half smile. "If you were a little older, I'd bet you a good cigar on this one."

Roger thought and then shook his head.

"He plays football for the University of Syracuse and he's twenty-one years old. What was your guess? About four or five?"

Roger nodded, licking his lips. He cleared his throat.

"If you think those are pretty bad, listen to this now," she flipped the switch and the tapes spun again. Roger tried to hear but couldn't make out anything. He looked at her as if to ask, Hey, what is this, some kind of a gag? But she returned his look with a patient smile and indicated he should still listen. He strained his ears but there wasn't a sound, he could swear to that. Nothing but the sound of the whirring tapes in their metal cases.

After another long moment, she looked at her wristwatch, then switched the machine off, and said quietly: "Of course, those are the worst kind. The kind that won't talk. Sometimes those that can, won't. And those that can't, simply cannot."

"Which one of them was that?"

She shrugged her heavy shoulders sadly. "I just played them both for you." She looked at some notes on the file cards in her hands. "The first one was a little boy of five. The second was a woman twenty-eight years old."

"What's it called? I mean—that?"

"Aphonia."

Well, he had never heard of that one. That was pretty bad, he thought, wondering how something like that could happen.

"I guess it's supposed to make me feel bet-uh," he said slowly, carefully. "But maybe they can't help it and they've got to talk that way—even the last kind that don't say anything."

Miss Clemm nodded, her mop of thick hair tilting downward now.

"I got no excuses. I *can* help it. I just got a lazy tongue."

Miss Clemm sighed a lugubrious sound.

"It's getting so there aren't any professional secrets any more," she said. "Everybody's got to get in the act." Then she hitched herself up in one vast churning movement. She waved her hand grandly, expansively, toward the green leather chair. "You're allowed to use the good furniture here. Do sit down and let's see if we can help each other."

Roger sat down, wondering why he wasn't nervous. *Maybe it's because she's so homely*, he thought.

Miss Clemm took out a white file card. "I guess we'll call you the Mystery Patient," she said.

"All I've got to do is tell you my name," he said. "Then you'll know, all wight."

He was suddenly aware of his last word and looked up to see her smiling gently at him. He couldn't help but look disgusted now. "You got it?" he asked.

"I got it," Miss Clemm said. "The mystery patient has an R problem." As Roger nodded, she said, "But you gave me a clue a little while ago." When he looked surprised, she reminded him, mimicking his voice. "I just got a lazy tongue," she repeated.

"Oh, yeah." He didn't mind losing this time.

Miss Clemm handed him the white card and a pen. "You can write it down for me, if you prefer," she said.

He shook his head and set his lips and she took the offerings away. "It's okay," he said. "I guess I need the—the—" he hesitated and looked at her. Miss Clemm pretended to be yawning. "Okay," he said. "*Pwactice*."

"Very well," Miss Clemm said. "Let's pwactice, then."

I guess they all do it, he thought. *Only they're not*

poking fun at you. They're only doing it to make you feel at home, you dummy. He looked at the tape recorder on her desk.

"Ahn't you going to put me down there?"

Miss Clemm shook her head. "It might be too awful," she said. "I might not want to be reminded."

"It's not that—*that* bad," he said. Then he became angry with himself for using the synonym. He was fed up with having to go around the Jonah words all the time. "It's not that *teh*-wibble," he said distinctly.

Miss Clemm's eyes didn't waver. "On the other hand," she said, "perhaps you *like* to talk that way. That first girl you heard on the recorder did."

"How come?" he asked.

"She found out she was more popular with boys when she used baby talk."

That was a new one, all right. There was no doubt at all about it. Everybody had their own problems.

"Well, I guess you want to hear my case hist—case hist—" he began. He noticed her face was very relaxed. She wasn't in any hurry to get this thing over with.

"You've evidently been to therapists before," Miss Clemm said. "You ought to know we don't finish sentences or complete words for people."

How come I forgot? Come on, don't be a dummy here. The rules and regulations here aren't bad.

"I'd say our theory is," Miss Clemm was saying, "that if you have a speech problem, then you have to make yourself say the words you fear. Then maybe some day you won't be afraid of them."

"If I just make myself?"

She nodded.

"What about those others—that last two? You said some could talk but won't. How come they won't?"

"Sometimes it's fear. Sometimes there's been an accident. Sometimes they're mad at the world and they won't give it another chance."

Hey, you dope, he told himself, *that's almost like you. And you can talk. So actually you're not so bad off.*

"Okay," Roger said. "All *wight*. Case hist-*owee*. And my name is W*a*-ja Bax-*tuh*. With the *ah* sound, I mean."

Miss Clemm was writing it all down on the white card.

"The funny thing is sometimes I can say it—I mean, sometimes I could say it—but then I'd lose it —only now I'm—wuss—like I backed up—and got wuss."

"What did they do?" she started to say and then she changed her mind. "Was it at home that you got it right?"

He shook his head.

"With another speech therapist?"

He nodded.

"Can you tell me something about what happened when you got the word right?"

I'm glad you reminded me, Roger thought.

"I got the big eyes," he said firmly.

Miss Clemm looked at him questioningly. Roger opened his eyes wide and pointed his finger at them, widening them as far as he could, remembering the

warm feeling he had experienced, wishing somehow
he could recapture it, if only for a little while.

Miss Clemm was nodding her head vigorously. Then
she was saying something to him with a slight smile.
But her voice faded. He was back in that other room
with the small-boned delicate teacher, that Miss Madison. . . .

"Growl, Roger—growl like a tiger." Her face
changed into a snarl and she was growling. "Like
this," she said, showing him her bared crooked
lower teeth.

"Gr-rrr!" he said. And then, "I got them that
time." He pointed at her eyes, opened wide with
delight, and was actually surprised. "You mean
you didn't open them on puh-puss?"

"Boy, you sure don't get any for that one. How
can you say puh-puss when you can growl like a
mean tiger?"

"I wish I was a tye-guh last night," he said, and
when she asked him why, he told her. The baby-
sitter had locked him in his room because he
couldn't pronounce her name: Brenda Bridges.

Her arms were around him instantly and he felt
her lips touch his hair. "The trouble with you,
Roger, is that you know too many mean people."

"How come you ain't mean?"

She smiled. "Oh, there are a lot of nice people
around. You just have to find them. And you will
some day, you'll see."

"Yeah, yeah. I'll bet," he said.

She leaned down suddenly with that odd jerky motion that reminded him of another child and picked up one of the wood blocks. Then she threw it with all her might across the room. The block crashed into the big gray mirror on the wall.

Now that's funny, he thought, *sitting in Miss Clemm's office. She hit the mirror. I just saw it crack. Back when it happened I thought she only hit the wall.* He remembered he had let out a delighted cry and whooped with joy, "Hey, how come you did that?"

"I was just mad enough. That's how come."

Then she had held out her hand. "Come on. It's too stuffy in here. I'll race you up to the ice cream building."

He was looking at Miss Clemm, now. She had a sparkle in her eyes, he noticed. *She's not so ugly!*

"That must have been a nice trip," she said. "Where'd you go?"

"Back to see Miss Madison," he said.

"I think it's nice to see old friends," she said.

"It'll be kind of tough for you with me," said Roger. "Because you can't examine my tongue. I mean inside."

"Oh?"

"You see, a long time ago, when I was a baby," he said and at the same instant he saw Roger Tunnell's stiffly held neck, as if he were standing beside him. He heard the quiet deep voice and felt again the warmth and intensity of the big man.

"I'll tell you what," he said. *A long time ago was*

*a long time time ago. Period. You couldn't stay a
baby forever.* "You got any of those tongue pwess-
uhs?"

"Yes. We got lots of them."

"Okay, then," he said leaning back in the big chair.
"Don't be afwaid. Take a good look."

"What?" she said, "and lose my mystery patient
right away? Gee, I don't know." She wagged her head
like a big dog, as if puzzled. "We don't have to do it
today."

"Oh, yes we do," Roger said. "We're way behind
all—all-weddy. Besides I got that Mistuh Walling on
my back. And he's nev-ah going to give up."

Miss Clemm frowned. "I think I know what you
mean. I imagine Mr. Rawling could be difficult in a
case like yours."

"Difficult?" Roger snorted. "He's not difficult. He's
the nation's numb-uh one comic. Wight after Jeh-wee
Jeeks," he added fiercely.

"If you want my opinion, he's just a stupid man. A
vain, stupid man," Miss Clemm said, her great jaw
outthrust.

Hey, you were right! Roger told himself.

"Anyway," he said, "I've got to twy—do somefing.
Some*thing!*" He looked at her disgustedly. "Sometimes that happens, too. Did you notice?"

She shrugged. "Nobody's speech is perfect all the
time. Remember, we're supposed to be human beings,
not machines."

"And sometimes I say my L's like my AH's. You
know, with W's instead."

"Perhaps you do," she said, her face intent and serious. "But it needn't continue."

"To get back to those wood tongue stickers," Roger said. "Like Miss Madison said—she was the one that gave me 'the big eyes'—she said it happened a long time ago when I was a widdle—a *little* boy. My mouth doesn't hut now. Maybe I can let you do what I couldn't when she—wanted to help me." He leaned forward, opening his mouth. "Go ahead. I won't make any scene this time. Honest."

Roberta Clemm heaved a deep breath and sighed heavily. "You'll be taking all the fun out of my work," she said.

CHAPTER TEN

ONCE IN A WHILE there was a present from his father. The box, bearing the imprint of an expensive shop in Beverly Hills, usually held some Hollywood-style sport shirt, so far out that he would have to be out of his mind to wear it. That was all he needed: to attract attention and then get involved in some dumb conversation. The less said, the better. He knew that.

Sometimes there was a letter, a brief one, dictated to the secretary. He could tell that from the initials at the bottom, right under his father's hastily sprawled signature. When money was enclosed, his father always mentioned that he hoped Roger could use this. *Boy, can I!* he always replied silently. It was a lot better than having to ask for it and get the third degree. It was better than the dole. The money from California was his secret fund, money he used for little things: a train ride down to Greenwich Village, admission to the planetarium at the Museum of Natural History.

When the secret mechanism silently rolled the tremendous roof back and the stars were projected, he sat in the darkness enthralled, while the heavens were unfolded for him and their mysteries explained by the lecturer. He hated the lights flashing on and ending the wonder of it. Then he got away as quickly as possible, ducking the ones he knew, not daring to be a part of any of the bantering groups that formed so easily and lingered for more casual pursuits, or headed for the pizza parlors, the ice cream parlors, Schraffts on Broadway for hamburgers and milk, record shops for the new hits, movies, window shopping, bus rides up to Fort Tryon park.

Aliens didn't use the buddy system. Aliens came and went on their own. Aliens didn't need anybody.

Anyway, it's only temporary. I'll have this problem licked soon and then I'll be able to mingle with the group and join in all those really great activities. I'll be so social it'll come out my ears.

Well, just when do you think this will happen? By the time they put somebody on the moon, do you think?

It'll happen, it'll happen; just stop bugging me.

Besides, we're making progress, don't forget that.

At least you gave her a chance to look in your stupid mouth. And now you know you're not one of those can't *people, those* aphoniacs. *Maybe you're a* won't *people but that's a lot better than being a* can't. *I mean, it shows we got a chance anyway.*

Growl like a tiger. That's all we've got to do.

We can say L, can't we? LLLLL, like that. Sure we can. Well, dummy, all we got to do is pull the lower jaw down slowly, like she said, until we reach the AH position—like this, stupid—LLLLL—ahhhhh—rrrrrRRR! Grrrrr—ahhhhh—rrrrrRRRR! You got it?

Or else we can imitate a church bell. All we've got to do is say Ding Dong, like that. Notice how that drops the jaw? Or we can say Caw Caw like a crow. Or Cock-A-Doodle-Doo like a rooster. Hey! You said it!

What else did she say? We've got to raise the tongue tip and cup it toward the palate only we don't touch it. Is that too difficult? Well, okay, so what if it is? We can go back to imitating church bells, DingDongDingDongDingDong, or bark or growl and we can practice saying Ouch because that drops the jaw, also. Ouch! Ouch! Ouch! You got that? Well, don't forget it!

And while we're feeling so good, what about that going to pieces in there? Well, we couldn't help that, she said. Those were just purpose tremors. They got a fancy name for it so you're not the only one that gets scared, dope. . . .

His face was pale and little beads of sweat appeared. He sat rigidly, arms tautly extended on the chair, hands clenched on the arm rests. His eyes were wide open, staring hard at the ceiling, while tiny tremors he could not control began to shake his body.

Miss Clemm was saying, "Now that's just dandy.

Only that's usually the way they look when they think I'm going to kiss them."

Roger shook his head, afraid to answer. His eyes filled with tears and suddenly brimmed over. *Oh, heck,* he thought desperately, *not again! Not now! Not any more.* Angrily, he brushed the errant tears from his face with his coat sleeve.

"I know it's dumb," he finally managed. "I thought it was all over." He looked down at his rigid arms and clenched hands and shook his head ruefully. "So what do I do now?" he asked her. "Maybe you ought to tell me to get lost."

Miss Clemm showed him the little wooden stick. "Is this really what you're afraid of?" Then, quite deliberately, she snapped it in half between her fingers, held out the broken pieces for him to see, then threw them into the waste basket.

"Now what'd you do that foh?" Roger demanded. "I'm weddy—honest I am. Don't mind this junk," he indicated his tensed body with a shake of his head.

Miss Clemm pushed back a thick clump of her hair. "I know you are. And you're a brave boy and I respect you for it—for what you're trying to do now."

"Yeah, yeah," he jeered.

"A person can be perfectly steady until he tries to accomplish his purpose. Then for some strange reason he'll start to quiver and shake. That's why we call it *purpose* tremors. My hand might be steady when I want to thread a needle. But when I go to put the thread through the narrow opening of the needle—my *purpose*—my hand will start to shake and my thread will miss. That's my purpose tremor."

"Sure, sure," he said mockingly.

What do I know about threading needles. I never tried it.

"The point I was trying to make," she said quietly, "was that the thing you were afraid of, the wooden stick of a tongue depressor, is broken now and quite useless. But you're still here. You were ready and you didn't break. You're still able to function."

Hey, he thought, *how about that?*

"Okay," he said. "Like you said, I'm still here. So let's get another one." He made himself slump and go limp in the big chair. He retracted his arms. Then he pushed his feet out and deliberately removed his hands from the chair arm rests, turning them over, palms up. "How's this, Doc?" he asked her.

"That's just fine," Miss Clemm said, bobbing her head vigorously. "But before I take that big look, perhaps you ought to know that there may be more to it than just finding a lazy tongue. Or a tongue that's not just right for talking correctly. Maybe you ought to tell me a little about yourself—your home life. How are things there?"

I'm real glad you asked me that, he thought, his hands clutching the chair spasmodically again. *My home life is really great, if you want to know. What home life are you talking about anyway?*

Instead he said tightly, his voice angry, "What's that got to do with it? I know a lot of kids wuss off than me and they don't act like babies."

"Perhaps they don't want to be babies," she said.

"It's the last thing we have to hold on to sometimes and we hate to give it up completely."

Oh, come on, what are you giving me?

"Because," her even voice continued, "if all of a sudden we are grown-up, there aren't any excuses any more and nobody to comfort us."

Sure, sure! I sure got an awful lot of that!

He saw in his mind's eye the great stone-faced stare and then heard the cold emotionless voice: "We'll take care of that later, Roger."

He could depend on his mother never to forget.

Then he saw his father pushing his chair away from the table as the telephone rang in his study, saying hastily, "That'll be for me."

Roger heard his own voice, thin and shrilling: "Tell him you got ya own baby!"

Well, there it was. So maybe this Miss Clemm was right. Maybe she had something there. *But I don't want to be a baby! It's not true. Okay, I said it, but it's not true.*

"Well, we ain't a big happy family now," he started explaining, and then he hesitated. Now he had a choice. He could try saying they broke up, or they separated, or they got divorced. He had to admit this time he couldn't walk around the words and pick other ones. The main ones this time all had the R's.

Instead he did it with his hands, throwing them apart. And evidently it was clear enough to Miss Clemm.

"And I imagine you're staying here with your mother?"

"Yeah."

"And do you write your father or speak to him on the phone? Does he keep in touch with you?"

His right hand unconsciously strayed to his pocket where the five dollar bill that had come in the morning's mail was. For some reason he couldn't explain he took it out of his pocket and showed it to Miss Clemm.

"We keep in touch," he said, "once in a while."

It was a little later on the Friday afternoon that he found himself using that particular five dollars from his father.

He had taken the subway downtown after school to walk around the section of New York where most of the artists and writers and creative people lived. Greenwich Village. The free-and-easy way the people dressed, the Bohemian atmosphere, the colorful shops, the odd-looking characters, the masses of movement, all fascinated him. Since first discovering this area Roger returned whenever he could.

It was only seven subway stops away, a ride that took twenty minutes, but it was like visiting another world. Uptown, where he lived, was considered "square." The villagers didn't wear neckties or jackets. Some of them, the more extreme, hippie types, wore beards.

Like the running man.

It was on Eighth Street at MacDougal, a corner usually noisy, crowded with strolling shoppers, villagers and tourists. This time it was so quiet you could hear the man in the blue dungarees breathing as he ran, and the sound of his sneakers slap-slapping the pavement.

Cars parked along each curb permitted only one-way traffic. People crowded the sidewalks in a thick unmoving line, just quietly watching.

They were part of a spectator sport, he found out later, one of the special village events, reserved for late Friday afternoons and evenings, when uptowners or other tourists started rubber-necking, exploring and crowding the village.

They were watching the Minetta Lane wolf pack in full cry.

Roger thought it must be a parade or something, to attract crowds like that. All he saw was a man running along in the gutter, not strange for a place like the village where all kinds of oddball things were supposed to happen.

Then he heard shrill hooting cries and five husky kids, wearing T-shirts, came running out of MacDougal Street and swung into Eighth. They appeared to be about fifteen years old and each carried a baseball bat. They were chasing the man in blue.

The people lining the curb didn't budge. And, somehow, on a street that ordinarily was very busy, there was no moving traffic at all.

The man in dungarees, Roger saw, was a very good runner and they probably never would have caught him as he swung up Eighth Street, heading east toward Fifth Avenue, a long block away. But suddenly another pack of yelling kids, carrying clubs, burst out of an alley on the south side, cutting him off.

Now the man was running back. He came closer and Roger could see his face through openings in the crowd. His skin was fair and freckled, his hair and chin whiskers red, his eyes were light blue. There was absolutely no fear in them. He seemed to be smiling but you couldn't be sure; he was gritting his teeth now with the effort of running, breathing hard.

The hundreds of grown-up people lining the curb, men and women, were all watching impassively, as if someone were flying a kite. As if nothing at all were happening.

As if a man weren't running for his life directly in front of them.

Now his sneakers were thudding almost in front of Roger. The running man turned his face to the crowd lining the sidewalk, and yelled:

"This is America, you mothers!"

The next instant, without trying to avoid it, he ran head-on into the first pack of toughs chasing him and disappeared from sight.

Roger heard dull thwacking crunching sounds but the grown-ups lining the curb were in his way and he couldn't see what was happening. He raced for some stone steps, feeling sick inside. When he was able to see over the heads of the people, the pack of toughs had the man in blue stretched out over the hood of a parked Ford Galaxie. He kept his arms over his head, trying to block the bats thudding down.

"We've got to do something," Roger heard himself saying.

Nobody moved. Nobody stirred to help.

Then a woman's scream cut through the awful dead air that held only the sound of heavy breathing and thudding blows. "Stop them, somebody! They'll kill him."

Well, I'm watching too, Roger thought. *I'm not helping much either.* His eyes blurred and he shook his head angrily.

Then an orange-colored taxicab came cruising up the street and stopped. The driver got out of his cab, a middle-aged husky man who needed a shave. He walked over to the fierce-faced young hoods and pushed the two nearest aside. He did it quite easily and slowly.

"Okay," he said, "Okay—that's enough now."

They looked at him surprised. Another he brushed back easily with his elbow, holding him off with his arm; then he reached over and picked the young man off the hood of the parked Ford. He held him close and the blood ran off the man's face on to the cabbie's shirt. He cradled the man in blue in his arms and Roger heard him say to the toughs:

"I said that's enough." His eyes looked at them steadily, unblinking, and they fell back, their sticks dropping slowly to their sides.

They danced back then, as if to regroup and charge, but suddenly one pointed off in the direction of the Avenue of Americas, Sixth Avenue.

"Fuzz!" he yelled. A police car was approaching. They all whirled as one, running toward MacDougal Street, hooting shrill happy cries. And then they were gone.

The cabbie held the young man up till the cruising squad car got there. Then he opened the door of his cab. He looked at the crowd lining the curb, filling the sidewalks, and there was contempt on his face. He made the gesture of spitting his contempt and disgust for them all before he got into his cab. Then he slammed the door, got his car into gear, and slowly drove up the street.

"*Ptoo! is right*," Roger thought.

As the black squad car moved in a straight line up the street, heading north, passing MacDougal without hesitating, without turning, the crowd dispersed, the solid knot of the curious dissolving into smaller, sometimes single units. They seemed unaffected. Some were already casually in conversation, picking up where they had left off. Some were actually smiling. *What are they, blind?* Roger wondered. *Are they deaf and dumb?*

How come nobody minded? How come nobody did anything? There were hundreds of people there. They couldn't all be relatives of the kids with the clubs. They couldn't all be neighbors.

I should have broken it up myself. I'm the only one who felt it like the cabbie. I should have done something.

Yeah, sure, you'd have scared them all right. They'd take one look at you and throw down their clubs and run. Sure, sure.

He looked down at his knees, surprised that the shaking tremulous feeling inside didn't show.

Yeah, you sure would have scared them all right.

He suddenly became aware of cars pressing the street-crossing stragglers, moving up inexorably like an assembly line. Where were you all before? he thought bitterly, seeing the street suddenly again alive with jostling, moving humanity. They all seemed to know where they were going. Right now he didn't. He noticed he was standing in front of a record shop, the loudspeaker broadcasting a new recording by one of the more popular young groups; The Dead Animals, he decided. Then he heard the words:

> "Something is happening
> And you don't know what it is,
> You want to know it better
> But all you get is this,
> That the feeling that you're thinking,
> Is that everything is stinking,
> And you *know* whatever's happening, *is*."

In his pocket his fingers rubbed the five dollar bill his father had sent. *This would be a good way to break it. That record was too good to pass up after what you just saw. Just in case I forget.*

He took a step toward the record store and noticed an old man approaching, dressed like a beggar, very tall, hatless, his hair thick and long, windblown over his shoulders. He wore an old army blanket cut out like a poncho; under that a striped dirty shirt, the sleeves cut short in a jagged line, and ragged tan shorts. Although it was a cold day his legs were bare, tan too, dirty and thin, and his bare feet were encased in worn leather sandals. He had a bushy unkempt gray beard and his dark eyes were sad and vacant. A small white placard was nailed to a long stave he carried. The sign read: PEACE.

He probably was another village custom because nobody paid any attention to him, though it was quite clear how tired he was. Roger looked down at his hand

and was surprised to see the five dollar bill there.

.He handed it, folded, to the bearded beggar as he passed. The old man didn't slow his shambling gait nor did he show any surprise. He merely nodded.

"Thank you, brother. Peace!" he said.

"Yeah," Roger said. "You can say *that* again."

CHAPTER ELEVEN

THE FIRST WINTER SNOW came early, catching the city by surprise, draping it with a feathery white blanket, to Roger's delight. He had seen snow before but only from a distance, on the high tops of the Sierra mountains outside Los Angeles. A lot of times on Old Baldy. This was the first he could walk in and feel. His spirits soared.

The cold accompanying wind had packed it high and solid on their outside terrace and he used all his strength pushing the door open to make his first snowball. His mother wanted to know what he was doing out there, letting the cold air in, getting himself wet. He told Her while he packed the snow hard. Then he sent his perfect ball flying in a high descending arc. The river wind got it and, from his perch high above Riverside Drive, Roger watched it explode in a puff of white crystals.

He yelled his delight. His mother got him inside before he froze up the whole apartment. The door didn't close properly now. Plainly it was all his fault.

"Okay," he told Her. "I'll play downstehs."

She yelled after him, telling him he was only going to get his feet wet, that he didn't have boots. But he went anyway. He was almost unable to contain his joy as he rode the elevator down to the street level. He managed this time to beat George, the elevator operator, to the revolving doors because George didn't share his enthusiasm for meeting the weather.

The snow was deep outside in the sidewalk drifts and he jumped and leaped upon them as if they were forts under relentless attack. He let himself stumble and fall, embracing the cold damp whiteness with his hands and body. He threw at least twenty more snowballs.

When he got upstairs again, his clothing was wet and his shoes were soaked. His mother reminded him that he had disobeyed Her, that now he would have to go to bed without his dinner. That was okay, it was worth it, he said, adding that She wasn't such a hot cook anyway and he probably wasn't missing much.

He was hungrier than he expected but didn't complain when She made Her own dinner. Later that night, after She had gone to bed, he got up and made himself a sandwich and sat in bed eating it, watching the snow fall outside his window. He took a hot bath so She wouldn't have the satisfaction of him coming down with a cold. He stayed up a long time watching the snow fill the dark city street.

From his corner window, facing the inner court, he could see a patch of Riverside Drive. Beyond it he felt the presence of the river, wide, dim, and mysterious. The soft glow of the street lights cast perfect circles upon the snow, each individually majestic, looking like so many little white islands receding in the distance, until they merged and disappeared into the infinite blackness of the night.

He sat up in bed, hugging his knees, staring out, lulled into a new kind of serenity by the enchantment of the flakes drifting and tracking across his window, covering the city so perfectly in their silent profusion.

It's like magic. I didn't know New York was supposed to be beautiful, too.

Then a wave of desolation and loneliness swept over him, engulfing him with sudden despair. *What's going to become of me?* he whispered to himself. He twisted and curled his body into a ball and buried his face in the pillow. As he waited for sleep to take him, he said impatiently, *Well, come on, dream.*

When he whirled out of the revolving doors of the high-domed lobby the next morning, he saw at once things were changed.

Hey, my snow, he almost wailed as he stood transfixed, *where's my snow?*

It was his first encounter with the hard-headed efficiency of the city's Department of Sanitation. All night, working like grim reapers, the trucks had removed the snow, leaving only gray dribbles. The ghostly white shining walls had become clumps of blackened rubble.

The maintenance crews of the apartment buildings on 86th Street had done their work well, too, shearing the snow from the sidewalks with their long-handled shovels and picks and ice scrapers, leaving only a thin irregular film of gray carpeting, lumpy and dull under his feet. A few cars parked along the street still wore their thick burgeoning white crowns and he found some satisfaction in those inviolate tops. Farther down the street, he came upon a truck from the Department of Sanitation, and in front of it a snow plow and bulldozer that pushed the snow from the moving traffic lane for the man to shovel into the truck. Roger looked at them bitterly. *Well, I suppose it's a job you've got to do but you could have waited a little.*

The green school bus was late and he danced and jigged on the corner of Park trying to keep warm. He'd need something else besides his sweater and jacket if this kind of weather continued, he decided.

Park Avenue had been cleared and traffic was moving along it as far as he could see. Looking up the hill to Broadway he saw traffic moving there, too. Then as his eyes swung to the left he noticed that the smaller side streets had been left unplowed. *Maybe they get to them later,* he thought. *Maybe I still got a chance for some fun.*

A few other stragglers his age arrived to wait for the bus, heavily bundled. Roger nodded, and then watched them throw snowballs at two girls who screamed and pretended panic. When the bus came there was a lot of boot stamping as they got aboard, and small pools of slushy snow ran along the aisles.

It was only a short ride to school but the city streets had not been entirely cleared and the bus slipped and skidded through snow clutters, bumping over the rock-like snow-fragmented corners. The girls on the bus squealed. Roger sat alone, spear-eyed, his head pressed against the cold pane, comforted by the hard time the bus was having, staring out at the still-white streets. *Well, I'm glad they left me something.*

He was even glad to see Mr. Rawling.

The Home Room class in Room 23 started his school day. Mr. Rawling was sporting clothing in keeping with the bad weather; thick ankle-high storm boots, red woolen socks, heavy brown wool slacks and a yellow vest under his brown and red-striped sport coat. Anyway, he's got good taste in clothes, Roger decided. Everything matches.

Mr. Rawling surveyed the meager turnout and sniffed. "I do suppose," he said acidly, "we'll have to take attendance and find out how many hothouse plants couldn't make it this morning." Several in the classroom tittered, looking proudly about. "Yes, my dears," added Mr. Rawling, "you all deserve medals. It was so brave of you to venture forth." A girl in the back laughed just a little too long. Mr. Rawling merely flicked his eyes at her and she subsided.

Baxter came quickly on the alphabetical rollcall and when he answered his "He-ah" loudly, Mr. Rawling lifted his eyes from the attendance sheet to regard him with feigned interest.

"I'm rather surprised that you could make it today, Baxter," he commented, "considering the elements. I was of the opinion that Californians derived thin blood from the sunny opulence of their climate."

"I didn't want to miss any of ya jokes," Roger heard himself saying. "My TV set is bwoke."

There was a distinct sudden intaking of breath from several in the class. Then a girl laughed clearly.

"Is that funny, Miss Johnson?" asked Mr. Rawling with a raw edge to his polite inquiry.

"Absolutely," the girl said. "At least, I thought so."

Roger tried not to show his gratitude. He might have known she would come to his rescue some day. It was the green-eyed blond he had accused of being the telescope peeper. She didn't look at him either.

Well, thanks, anyway.

The class started to buzz and the atmosphere to change. Heads were turning in Roger's direction. He looked up once and saw furtive smiles. *Oh, come on; not again. Forget it.*

Mr. Rawling rapped on his desk. The buzzing stopped. The head turning stopped. They waited in awe for the king, who had been assailed, to strike him dead.

"I'm sorry to disappoint you all," he said. "I happen to agree with Miss Johnson." There was a nervous titter from the class. "*Touché*, Baxter!" he added and then went on with the roll call. When he came to the J's and called, "Marion Johnson," she replied "I'm here," and he said wryly:

"Don't I know it!"

They all laughed. He had won them again.

Well, he took it like a good sport, Roger thought, *but don't worry. You'll pay for that crack yet. He'll get even. You watch and see.*

Surprisingly, his defender was waiting for him in the hall when they changed classes. She greeted him with a warm smile. *As if we're old friends.*

"I guess we're both dead now," she said laughing.

"I don't keh," he said.

Then he remembered he had said that the other time and she had mimicked him. And when he had asked were they still playing the game, again exposing his inability to pronounce the R, she had answered, "Nope. It's time for a little work now."

He took a deep breath. *Come on, try it, try it!* "I don't care," he heard himself say.

"That was a good one," she said quickly, perceptively.

Disarmed, he couldn't keep a fleeting smile from passing over his face.

"Too bad you had to give him the satisfaction of the other word," she said, moving away slowly down the hall.

He took two quick steps and caught up. "What one?" he asked and as she reminded him, he remembered. "Bwoke." He never would have believed that he could laugh with somebody about it.

"I bet you can say it now," she said.

He nodded confidently. "Bwoke," he said.

I just had it, he silently moaned inside. But the rage mounting within him was suddenly checked by her expression. Something about it seemed to mirror his emotion.

"I understand it takes a while before you can get to depend on it," she said.

Now how did she know that?

"Anyway, if you think about it," she continued, in her crisp level voice, "everybody's got the same problem, more or less. I mean, even those who can speak well—without any speech defect, that is."

"Okay," he said. "I give up."

"One way or another, it's all communication, isn't it? We're all trying to communicate—to break through with somebody—so we can understand them."

He thought about that and liked it.

"Hey, how come you talk like that?" he hurried to ask. They were near the end of the hall now and would have to separate for different classes.

"Talk like what?" she asked.

He couldn't think of words and had to tap his head, feeling foolish. But he persisted. "I mean—not how you say it but *what* you say."

"Oh, that! It's easy. My father is a psychiatrist." She rolled her eyes and tapped her own head, adding, "Besides, I was an only child."

She gave him a smiling farewell wave and turned into the room at the end of the corridor, leaving him flat on his heels, feeling like a lump. The small sign on the door she entered read:

FRENCH

You might know it. She takes a foreign language, too.

In science class his mind kept snapping back to her. *That's a cool crazy girl. You know, it wouldn't hurt if you got a little intelligent, too. I mean, that way maybe you could even carry on a conversation without having to tap your head like some kind of a moron.*

The science teacher finally reached him before class was over. He looked at the little scrap of paper where he had written:

30,000,000,000,000,000

The number of molecules in a quart of water, stupid, he reminded himself. *So anyway, now, any time you feel small you know there's something a lot smaller around. And I think Mr. Kline said also that there are more molecules in a quart of water than there are quarts of water in all the oceans of the world! It's about time we knew things. We gotta hurry it up a little here.*

The rest of the day at school he felt different, as if the iceberg hidden deep within him was thawing or breaking up. He remembered all the dates and events he had to for history and Miss Donovan seemed pleased. It was just a relaxed kind of a day, he told himself. The teachers seemed friendlier and he felt more at ease. *Maybe it's the snow. It certainly could be the snow. I sure can't think of anything else to make this big change in everything. Maybe everybody's happier. Including me.*

The school cafeteria was not as crowded as usual because of all the absentees, but it seemed noisier, more boisterous. He brought his hamburger and potato chips and carton of milk to the side where he usually sat, apart from the group, and wolfed them. Then, instead of leaving abruptly and finding a quiet corner to read in, he stayed, pretending to read, listening to them, lulled by their animation and good spirits into a rapport he couldn't understand. He even found himself actually smiling at some of the conversation.

Suddenly aware, he froze but he didn't let it pass.

Come on. Let's keep our eyes and ears open for a change. Let's find out who everybody is, for once. I mean, it's not like you got to be a stranger here all the time. After all, you practically live here, you know. Five days a week. Every day practically.

He felt pretty good until he remembered that his next class was English. It could be Rawling's revenge, he thought, and licked his lips.

Well, we'll find out soon enough. Maybe the snow softened him up like everybody else. And while we're at it, let's try not to give him another word like "bwoke." Let's practice on a couple of those R sounds so maybe this time we'll get it right and then maybe he'll get off our back.

Okay. There's race and ran and rapid. He ran a rapid race. He ran a rapid race. Who ran a rapid race? I ran a rapid race, that's who. And who are you? I mean, what's your name?

I know my name. Don't you bug me now.

I know you know it but can you say it?

Roger. That's my name.

Hey, that's very good! Now do us both a favor and see if you can say it out loud.

"Roger," he said.

Roger, I love you.

The river is wet. The car is a wreck. The ship is far from shore.

What else?

The window is broken. Broken.

Let's do it once more for the east coast.

"It's *broken*," he said.

Now try to remember that. Don't lose it. Grass

*grows and there are pretty flowers and France is a
country where they speak French.*

And I wish I could, he added to himself.

He was lucky. Mr. Rawling found some blood to
draw from another source. Roger felt sorry for the
gangling boy standing up front near Mr. Rawling's
desk. The teacher was holding a small slip of paper in
his hand, his face passive, his expression gentle. He
waited until the English class had settled into its seats
and the room grown quiet. Then his voice purred the
sentence.

"This note states that you are late because you
were unable to get the car started." He held the note
at arm's length now, between two fingers. "Is that
correct, Appleton?"

The boy nodded. He was very tall and very thin,
with a pronounced stoop to his shoulders.

Aware, as always, when he had the complete attention of the class, Mr. Rawling proceeded. He tapped
the note. "Unable to get the car started! You? Am I
to assume that you were intending to drive the vehi-
cle?" He smiled archly and the class began to titter.

"N-no, sir," Appleton said, shaking his head vio-
lently.

"Ah, then," said Mr. Rawling, still purring, "may
I inquire *who* was unable to get the car started?"

"Th-the chauffeur, s-sir," said the boy.

When Mr. Rawling, with exquisite timing mouthed
the word "chauffeur?" with open mouth and rolled
eyes, the class responded with a roar of laughter.

Oh, boy, thought Roger mirthlessly, *that's funny.
That's really funny. That's a big laugh, all right.*

"Your chauffeur couldn't get the car started, is that it?" asked Mr. Rawling innocently.

The discomfited boy nodded again, his throat gulping nervously.

"*Your* chauffeur or the family chauffeur?" continued Mr. Rawling, warming on his quest.

Appleton tried to smile at this. "The family's, sir."

Mr. Rawling smiled gently in return. "Oh, that's nice. That's very proper. I'd hate," he added after a slight pause, "to learn that one of my own seventh graders had his own personal chauffeur. I think that would be going just a little too far. Don't you agree, Appleton?"

"Y-yes, sir."

"Possibly when you're in the ninth—" but Mr. Rawling didn't have to finish the sentence as the class roared.

Roger writhed in his seat. He looked around at the faces contorted with laughter and gritted his teeth. *I don't get it. What's so funny?*

Mr. Rawling folded the note and put it in his notebook. Young Appleton looked, shrugged, decided the inquisition was over and started to walk off to his seat. He was stopped by Mr. Rawling's voice. "Just what kind of car do you have that your family chauffeur was unable to get started, Appleton?"

The boy flushed. The laughter mounted. Mr. Rawling waited, lips pursed, arms folded indolently on his desk.

Don't tell him, Roger was silently urging the boy. *Don't give him the satisfaction. Just don't answer him.*

But you'll have to, I guess. I sure hope you got a good one.

"A Rolls," the boy mumbled.

Roger was delighted. *Attaboy!*

But Mr. Rawling evidently had not heard, the laughter of the class working against him this time. "A what?" he asked, petulantly.

The Appleton boy, standing limply against the radiator, started to answer but couldn't get the words out. Roger saw his lips moving spasmodically and his own eyes started to twitch. There seemed to be a red film over them. He tried brushing it away. He blinked and it was still there.

Then he was on his feet, his books crashing down on the floor, everybody looking at him. He was leaning forward, his weight balanced on hands not open and spread but balled into fists. *What's going on here?* he wondered. Then he heard a voice shrilling from what seemed a great distance. *Hey, is that me?*

"He said it's a Rolls Royce! You get it?"

Then he was sitting down, feeling the silence around him. Mr. Rawling was looking at him intently, coolly. Something was puzzling him, Roger suddenly knew. Then . . . of course! Mr. Rawling had discovered he'd used the R sound!

"Would you mind repeating that, Baxter?" he asked.

Well, now you did it, birdbrain, he told himself.

He sat hunched over, his eyes flicking about the class, not certain what he was looking for, at first. Then, as he noted each face, he knew. The faces were hostile. As if he'd spoiled all their fun. He kept looking, noting each in turn, and then he saw *her* seat was empty. *That's too bad. Because I sure wouldn't mind seeing a friendly face right now. I guess maybe she was smart enough to cut this class, or maybe she had to see the nurse about something.*

Well, that's too bad, Jack, but I think we got enough worries right here without worrying about that Marion Johnson.

Evidently he had missed one.

"I'll ask you once more, Baxter, to repeat that," said Mr. Rawling. Then he added acidly, contemptuously, "providing of course that you can."

Oh, come on, Roger told himself, *is that you on your feet again? What are you, some kind of a jumping jack, Jack?*

Then he heard himself say: "I know a better one. He's funny, too. Jerry Jeeks!"

He jerked his head at a loud clanging noise, swooped down for his books and didn't look back. *Saved by the bell! Maybe they'll shoot you tomorrow but right now you don't have to stay in this crummy place.* As he left he could have sworn he heard some cheers. *Yeah, I'll bet! I think your hearing is rotten, too.*

CHAPTER TWELVE

IT WAS COLD walking home but he was wound up and didn't feel the wind. He noticed everybody was wearing overcoats; some were swathed in mufflers.

I'd like one of those long and woolly ones; in red and white peppermint stripes.

He saw a boy his age wearing one outside his short winter coat and it looked great. *I guess I'll need a winter coat like that one too. I don't think She'll give me a big argument about that. After all, She hates colds. She'll get me the coat, I'm pretty sure of that. Oh, She'll fret and complain but I guess maybe She'll worry about how it would look for Her own son to be walking around in the winter without a coat like She couldn't afford it, living on Riverside Drive and Her husband—well, Her ex-husband—a big Hollywood producer. No, don't worry, She'll get you the coat.* He looked down at his feet scuffing the hardened snow. They were getting cold. *She'll get you boots, too. Don't worry. They'll be expensive ones too like that Appleton kid was wearing.*

His mind leaped back to the inquisition in afternoon English class. He wondered if Mr. Rawling would have asked Appleton if they were too poor to afford a second car or a third car. And what kind were they, if they had them.

His eyes sparkled. What if it had got to that and the Appleton kid told Rawling their second car was a Bentley which the *other* chauffeur was using to take his baby sister to kindergarten? That would have killed him.

The thought of the Bentley reminded him of Pat Bentley, the knockout model who lived in the penthouse. He hadn't seen her lately. She'd get a big kick out of what happened today, mostly about him finally saying the R's. Boy, he'd had a break there for a change. It could have come out *Wolls Woyce* or *Jeh-wee Jeeks* and then he'd have been dead for sure.

He remembered the expensive cars his father had owned. Too bad that comic Rawling didn't ask him about them. That would have been good for lots of humor. The Eldorado, for instance; that big black Caddie job he's driving now isn't so special. But before that were the red Ferrari, and the Jag, the MK IX. And before that the dual Ghia, the same kind that Sinatra had. And what did She have? Well, the last one was that quiet purring Facel Vega, the one She had customized with the special leopard skin upholstery interior. He never felt comfortable in that car. Leopards could bite you.

He remembered driving with Her to that designer

of the far-out cars in North Hollywood. He could still see the big sign with the script letters that practically yelled at you: THE KUSTOM KING.

The small stocky balding man had been directing a spray lacquer job on a cut-back Lincoln when they pulled up, and didn't come over until he had a chance despite Her fretting and drumming on the wheel. Then She was asking him what could be done with it and the man grinned crookedly and scratched his head.

"I dunno," he finally had said. "You're in this car for about twelve *thou* now. You wanna try for another ten?"

He whistled, remembering. Twenty-two thousand for a car? You could almost buy two Rolls for that kind of money. His father had gotten a little heated up about it when he heard the glad news.

"You're nuts. Absolutely nuts."

That was all he had said.

Come to think of it, we must be rich, he told himself.

You mean were, dumbbell.

Okay, so we were. But there's probably something left. Didn't I hear Her saying something to somebody recently about that California property settlement law thing where they get half of whatever there is?

Okay, so that means you'll get the overcoat and boots you need for this kind of weather. Plus the red and white muffler. If you make a big stink about it.

He remembered another car the Kustom King had made. . . .

It came roaring into their driveway, tires spitting gravel as it screamed to a stop. There was a loud honking and the sound of guns being fired and over it all, fitting somehow, a wild cowboy yell. It sounded like somebody was out there stampeding cattle. In *Brentwood*, Los Angeles!

He followed his father outside and there was the longest shiniest car he had ever seen. It was an all-white convertible trimmed with silver and gold and glistening stones that looked like diamonds.

A giant of a man stepped out of it, a cowboy dressed all in white from his broadbrimmed Stetson to his narrow high-heeled buckskin boots. He towered over Roger's father, big and broad and sturdy as an oak, his face as seamed and furrowed and weather-beaten. There was fancy stitching around the collar and pockets of his white shirt, and his wide belt had a thick silver buckle. His boots had silver spurs and silver zippers on the sides. When he shook hands with Roger it was like being held by a big steel shovel.

He was as hearty and good natured as Roger thought a giant should be, his laughter coming easily in a full-throated roar. He picked Roger up, held him high in the air and walked him around the car holding him flat as if he were flying.

The door handles on the outside were pearl-handled six-shooters. On each side of the sweeping fenders were long thin gold rifles. Sharply pointed and curving over the hood were the great ivory horns of a long horn steer. The rear reflector lights were mounted on large gold spurs. The spare wheel was mounted on twin sets of ivory horns, and encased in white calf. There was a silhouette picture in curling black lines of a cowboy riding a bucking bronc. The man's name was there in writing: HOOT HOLIDAY.

The cowboy opened the door and held him now in the palm of his big hand, level without a tremor, as if he were a tray. He eased Roger inside where the boy could see and smell the leather. The door openers on the inside were fancy spurs, the armrests goat horns. The carpeting was goat fur, the sunshade white calf. The bucket seats were of white leather in the front and those in the rear spotted like the Appaloosa.

Ten little horse heads in silver and gold decorated dashboard and doors, instead of the usual lighter, choke, windshield wiper, lights and ignition. The gear shift was another silver six-shooter. The big cowboy pulled the trigger for him and instead of a gunblast the doors opened. Then, when he saw that the boy would like it, he dumped Roger gently on the back seat, laughing when he saw his delighted eyes.

"It ain't hardly a hoss, son," he said, "but it packs a heap more livin'!"

His father's voice was thin with dismay.

"You didn't sink all I paid you for the picture on this—*creation*, did you, Hoot?"

The big cowboy laughed some more and took his hat off. His hair was long and a thick lock of gray fell in front of his steel gray eyes. He mopped

his tan brow with thick fingers and snapped the
sweat away. He put his hat back on his head at a
jaunty angle and turned, surveying the car. Then
he spoke to the little boy rolling around inside
putting his happy face into the soft bold-colored
patches.

"You like it, son?"

Roger nodded happily, unable to speak, gulping with the joy of this wonderful moment.

"Well, *did* you, Hoot?" the father persisted.

The big man pouted a little and dug into the
gravel with his boot. "Now, pardner, don't you
get riled up at ol' Hoot." He wheeled again and
looked proudly down at the gleaming car. "Ain't
she a beauty?"

His father was frowning. "How much?" When
the man didn't answer but just stood there grinning happily, the father snapped: "They didn't
want you at all in the front office. I had to pull a
lot of wires to get you the part. And you had to
blow it all on this? What if you don't get another
job? You're too old for the rodeos now, friend.
And if that picture doesn't make money, you're
washed up."

"As bad as that, eh, *amigo?*" the cowboy said,
his broad carefree smile fading and a little twisted.

Don't talk like that to him, he wanted to tell
his father but his father kept talking, spitting out
short bursts of words as if he were shooting at the
big cowboy standing there almost helpless. The
grin was only pasted on now and his steady gray
eyes were unsmiling.

He tapped the six-gun handle. "This here is real silver." He kicked his white buckskin toe at the rifles. "Solid gold plate," he said.

"Solid like your head," his father said. "How much?"

The cowboy's long arm reached inside the beautiful car and picked Roger out and set him softly on his feet. The big rough hand rumpled his hair gently.

"*Adios, chico*," he said. He stooped and slid behind the wheel. "Ah figgered it was worth the thirty thousand," he told Roger's father in a soft drawling voice. "It made ol' Hoot happy."

"You can be happy in a Chevy," Mr. Baxter said grimly.

"Reckon so," said the cowboy. "*Adios*," he waved and the car started and the wheels spun, shooting gravel as he gunned the big motor. He roared down the curving drive and when he came near the end swung the wheels left and drove deliberately into the white stone wall there as if he wanted to go through it. He got out of the ruined car slowly when they got there and started to walk away. His father ran up and grabbed his arm, asked why, why? and the cowboy looked down at him and said he'd taken all the fun out of it.

Roger wished he could come to school in a car like that. Just for the look on Mr. Rawling's face.

What he didn't get though was the laughing, his mind leading him back to the incident at school. It's a private school so everybody is supposed to have money. And that Appleton kid's old man is the owner of that big department store on Fifth Avenue.

So that makes him a millionaire's kid, at the very least. So naturally there's going to be a chauffeur, right? With all old man Appleton's probably got on his mind, is he going to drive his own car to work and sweat out the parking problem?

He shook his head. *I don't get it,* he thought disgustedly. *What difference did it make if it was a private car or a taxi or a bus or the subway, even? They're all rich kids. Why was it so funny? And how come they all acted like I spoiled all their fun when I interrupted? Like I took away their candy or something, for God's sake.*

He could see again the skinny gangling boy bobbing his head, unable to answer Mr. Rawling. *I bet that kid's got trouble home, too. I bet his old man, with all that dough he's got, doesn't like his kid bobbing his head around like that, like it was an apple on a stick. I bet if that keeps up Miss Clemm's going to have another customer.*

He was almost home before he realized he hadn't really appreciated the snow along the way. *I've got to watch it or Rawling's going to spoil whatever fun I've got left.*

Crossing Park Avenue he found it almost completely cleared; only a thin surface coat of snow remained. Then he remembered the small side streets north of his apartment house.

There was still snow on 87th Street, and cars parked in the street overnight were covered with it, the own-

ers not even having bothered to clear a space to them.
Some would be frozen and wouldn't start now. A lot
of Appletons here, he thought. Without chauffeurs.
This was the do-it-yourself block.

The buildings along this street were almost uni-
formly three-storied, occasionally four, and called
brownstones, although for the most part they were
dingy red or sooty black. Their distinctiveness lay in
their high stoops, usually fifteen or twenty steps with
black metal railings. Narrow paths had been gouged
out of the snow, some trampled down, a few completely cleared, so that he could count the still-wet
steps.

An occasional sign advertised apartments for rent,
furnished and unfurnished; others, single rooms; some
were mute requests for trade. A small dirty gray one
read: PIANO LESSONS. Another, TAILOR. ALTERATIONS.
He passed two M.D. signs and one CPA. The sound
of a wailing dog came from behind a small black sign
on an ornate metal stake, reading: DR. RUDOLPH
MESILLON, VETERINARIAN.

*I sure wouldn't want to be a dog cooped up in
there. Where would I run?*

All the buildings had basement apartments. He
opened a gate, and under the high arched stone entrance was a small sign over a black button encased
in brass. It read: RING FOR SUPT.

He liked this street. It seemed more homelike. It
was wide enough for two lanes but the city ordinance
signs high on their granite posts said: ONE WAY
STREET. His street, a block south, had four lanes, per-
mitting in addition the traffic of crosstown buses.

Apart from a girl walking far ahead, he was the only person moving on the street. Obliquely across from the corner he was approaching rose a big, black, ugly, twelve-story building, a large sign on its roof announcing—Hotel with River View Apartments, Suites, Restaurant, and Coffee Shop. It squatted there in dreary outmoded splendor, one part of its L on 87th Street, the rest on Riverside Drive.

What a dump, he thought, wondering what kind of people would want to live there. *Maybe it's for the river view. Otherwise it sure looks depressing.* He thought back to some of the fantastically beautiful hotels he had seen in Los Angeles, Brentwood, and Beverly Hills, cantilevered like much of the modern architecture there, swooping out into space as if taking big extra gulps of air. There hadn't been one as ugly as this. He could see in his mind's eye their tropical settings: the yucca and tall evergreens, citrus and cactus, acacias with their fernlike fingers, the palms and palmettos, broad-leaved banana trees, the pepper and eucalyptus. And the rock gardens with their groupings of primrose and dwarf pines, hyacinth, calla lilies, birds-of-paradise, the purple verbena and glossy ivy, thick and luxuriant. He'd almost forgotten how beautiful it was back there.

He remembered the orange and fig and seedling avocado, the yucca with their flowering white lily clusters, that surrounded his *own* house back there. *I guess you gave up a lot,* he thought, engulfed suddenly by a wave of nostalgia . . .

*He was up in the small orange tree and She
wanted him to come down.*

At once, Roger. You'll fall.

Aw, no, Ma. I just want that one.

*You silly fool. There are five hundred others
exactly like that one right down here, right near
my arm. I can pick any I want and so can you.*

I just want that one, Ma.

*You're going to fall down and hurt yourself.
You'll break an arm or a leg. Come down this
instant, Roger, do you hear? Your father is too
busy to take time off to rush you to a hospital
and I have a million people coming for dinner.
Now for the last time, will you get down—*

And then he fell.

Now again he saw himself falling, bumping against
the twisted branches that lashed his face. He tried
to catch hold but somehow he couldn't grip any of
them long enough and then as he was plunging head-
first to meet the ground he saw Her face somehow,
the smile on it, the nodding head, and heard the
high thin words framed in malice: *I told you you'd
fall, Roger.*

*Well, I guess I made Her happy for once, that
time.*

CHAPTER THIRTEEN

His FEET suddenly hit a slick frozen spot in the snow lumping the 87th Street sidewalk, and he almost fell.

Hey, it looks like everybody's doing it. Straight ahead down the street the girl also walking along in the lonely cold was falling, too.

She was about forty yards ahead. She appeared to tilt, as if in slow motion, her arms flailing circularly and her red mittens blurring, and then her black boots flashed in the late afternoon sun as her feet went out from under her. He heard her hit the walk with a crunch. She lay there, her body twisted.

When he came skidding up, her face was down in the foot-stomped snow. He extended his hand to help her up, and noticed it was blue with the cold.

"You okay?" he asked.

He heard her muttering. She propped herself on her arms, untwisted and sat up, wiping the snow from her face. Then she looked up, saw his extended hand, but made no move to take it.

He was still leaning down over her. "Can I give you a hand?" he asked and she shook her head, almost angrily, he thought. Her eyes were the coldest blue he had ever seen. Her face was pale, almost white, and there were angry red splotches where she had rubbed the snow off. Again she shook her head and her long blond, almost white, hair bounced.

"I can manage, thank you," she said.

"Okay," he said, backing off.

She closed her eyes and leaned back. Then she threw her weight forward, got to her knees and with a sudden galvanized jerk was standing there, tottering and unsteady.

"Well, you made it," he said, for lack of something better to say. Her eyes were frosty. It was as if she didn't see him. *Okay*, he thought, *so what? I just wanted to help*.

The girl suddenly took another step forward and before he could move and grab her she was down again. This time her muttering was louder and she pounded the hard snow with her mittened fist.

Before he could think, Roger had his hand under her arm and got her back on her feet.

"I said I could manage," she said in a low voice, her eyes still frosty, her hands busily knocking off the snow from the back of her coat.

Roger shrugged. "Okay," he said. "So manage."

He turned away, figuring *The heck with that*, and started walking. The canopy of the north wing of his apartment house was directly ahead and although he had never yet used that entrance decided he would now. He cast a quick look over his shoulder to see how this mean-mannered girl was doing, just in time to see her wobble and go down again. *Oh, well*, he shrugged, running back to her.

This time she was sitting there as if waiting for him, though her eyes were still hostile. He extended his hand again, wondering if she might bite it. She took it, and was on her feet once more, brushing herself off. Roger stayed close, his hand still on her arm. After a few tentative steps, she still had trouble maintaining her balance, and he walked along slowly beside her, looking down at her knee-high black rubber boots. *They ought to give her some traction.*

"Maybe you ought to get rid of those boots," he said. "I think they're making you walk like you're cwippled."

There, he lost the R sound again! he thought bitterly. Her eyes were on a point far ahead. Well, maybe she didn't catch it. He hoped.

She said, "As a matter of fact, I *am* crippled."

Huh? he thought. *Did I hear right?*

"I can't walk decently even if there *isn't* any snow," she was saying in a matter-of-fact voice.

Oh, brother, that's great! You really opened your mouth real good that time.

"I was only kidding," he said, feeling very warm all of a sudden, wishing he could disappear.

Surprisingly, she smiled. "I know," she said. "You wouldn't have said it, otherwise."

He nodded his head vigorously, gulping.

They had reached the blue canvas canopy of the apartment house now and she gripped the cold brass post supporting it. "Saying cripple is like saying cancer, it seems," she said. "It's a taboo word."

I got lots of them, too, he thought instantly. But his mind leaped to her problem again. What was the matter with her, and if she was crippled why would she be out walking in anything as treacherous as snow? And how come she doesn't have a crutch if she's crippled?

He noticed suddenly that her red-mittened hand was pointing across the street and he realized that she was saying something about the coffee shop in the hotel over there being open and didn't he feel like something warm now. He nodded happily and took her arm again and this time she didn't tell him she could manage.

In one of the little booths with the kind of wonderful worn-smooth wood tops he loved, they ordered coffee and doughnuts, for which she insisted she would pay because it was *her* idea. Okay? her eyes asked and he merely shrugged and smiled. He felt pretty good. The pert chubby waitress moved quickly for her age, and when the warm mugs came he kept his hands wrapped around his a long time before lifting it to his lips.

It all started with an automobile accident, she told him. "This Christmas will be my second anniversary," she said without bitterness now. Her legs had been crushed. A cousin whom she loved had been with her. "She was killed. I was luckier."

Yeah, sure, he thought. *That's luck, all right.*

The doctors had finally brought the crushed legs back to life. "The only trouble is," she frowned, "one leg grows faster than the other. That's why I have to have so many operations. To keep me from growing up all lop-sided." Then, with almost a grin, no frost in her eyes now, she asked, "Guess how many I've had so far?" And when he shook his head, not wanting to guess, she told him. "Fourteen."

"Fuh-teen?" he repeated, not caring about losing the R sound with her. It didn't seem that important.

Look, he wanted to say, *being crippled isn't so bad.* But he knew it was a lie. *I'm a cripple, too, in a way. Just listen to the way I talk.* But he didn't tell her that either. He didn't say anything, because what could he say that would mean something?

He thought of how right that girl Marion Johnson had been in using the word communication. If you didn't communicate, not only couldn't you break through with anyone, you couldn't even start.

His mind wandered to a writer friend of his father, supposed to be very talented but who drank too much. Once the writer had come over and visited with his father. In the study where they had gone to talk he heard the clink of glasses and later heard the visitor's voice loud and angry, then a sound like a chair falling over. The writer had gone angrily out to his car in the driveway, revving it very high, wildly screeching his tires as he backed off, taking the whole curve in reverse at a speed he'd never heard there before, just zooming out of the place and away, backward. When, later, his mother had asked his father if he'd given the writer the assignment to do the new picture, he remembered his father shaking his head and saying no, he couldn't give it to a cripple.

He remembered himself not understanding. . . .

"I saw him walk in. He could walk fine."

His father gave him a crisp tolerant smile. "Being crippled doesn't apply just to walking. Some people are crippled by their own bad habits—they don't function the way they should."

"Why don't Mr. Gowdy function?"

"Because he has a bad habit and it comes in a bottle."

"You mean he dwinks?"

"It's not just that he—drinks, Roger. It's that he can't stop drinking. And when that affects his work, so it's no longer responsible, then it's bad."

"But he's such a nice man."

"Yes, he is. And so are a lot of other drunks."

"So how come he wote all of those books you got?"

His father picked up some papers, as though he were getting tired of the questions. "I guess he wrote—wrote, Roger, not wote—you've got to get those R's straight, son—anyway, he wrote the books before he developed this bad habit. Once you start leaning on the bottle, you're as good as dead."

"But—"

"Sorry, son, but that's all I have time for. I have to make a few calls—" the door closing on

him. He guessed his father was calling another writer who didn't have such a bad habit.

The scene dissolved in his mind and he saw the white-faced girl opposite him. She was saying something and he wanted to listen. He even looked like he was listening but his mind was away again and he was back in the classroom looking at Mr. Rawling, hearing the bite in his voice, the well-bred sneer masked by his capable vocabulary. He felt there was something a little wrong with Mr. Rawling but he didn't know what it was. The other girl, Marion Johnson, had said he was a sadist. He wasn't too sure what that was. Then he heard the sudden intake of breath of the class and he was looking at them again, one by one, seeing the open hostility and hate in their faces. *For what? Just because I spoiled their fun? And what kind of fun is that anyway?*

I guess maybe one way or another we're all crippled.

The girl opposite set her mug down. "—and I transferred here and go to this school of music," she was saying.

He shook his head, wondering how much he'd missed. He was reluctant to ask which school, in case she'd already told him while his mind was leap-frogging.

"Well, how come you walk to school on a day like this?" he asked, hoping she hadn't already explained that, too.

"I like to pretend once in a while that I'm normal."

Yeah he thought. *That's always a good idea.*

She opened her bag and surprised him by taking

out a crumpled pack of cigarettes, looking at him coolly. Then she lit one and blew out smoke.

"I'm not going to ask if you smoke," she said. "I know a lot of kids do. But I don't have to sneak away to do it. When you have my problem, you can get away with a lot of things. That is, if you have sympathetic parents, I guess."

Yeah, maybe that's the clue. He wondered if he'd be permitted to smoke if he had his legs operated on all the time. *No, I guess not. There'd be a lot of reasons but I can guess right now what the answer would be.*

"Is it because ya legs—huht?" he asked. He had lost the R's, that was a fact. And he didn't have time to practice any cock-a-doodle-doos or growl like a tiger or make like a bell right now, either, he thought savagely.

"I guess that's part of it," she admitted. "At least it takes my mind off the moaning and groaning. And feeling sorry for myself. You know."

He shoved his notebook across the pitted wooden table between them. She looked surprised and he pointed a finger at his name written there. "That's my name. And I can't say it. I can't do the AH sound. That's mostly what I do *my* moaning—and gwoaning about."

She grinned widely. "You won't have any problem with mine. Nemo Newman. Can you do N's?"

He nodded, relieved. "Nemo Newman," he said.

"Actually," she said, "I really feel sorry for people who can't talk decently. I'm lucky not to have that problem. My problem is I can't shut up."

He managed a weak smile and felt a dull pain in his ankle.

"And if you want to know why I just kicked you, that's to remind you not to feel sorry for me. I can't stand sympathy. As a matter of fact, I don't know any cripple who can."

"Okay," he said. "I only feel sow-wee for my ankle."

"That time I only kicked you with the bad leg so regard that as a warning. *Par avance*," she added.

Everybody knew French but him. "What does that mean?"

"In advance. I can curse in French, too. Want to hear me?"

"What's the good if I don't know what it means?" he asked. He liked the way she went on and on. For a crippled girl, she sure was animated. Like a wound-up top.

"We could go out together sometime," she said casually. "I assume you live in the neighborhood and all we'd need would be our parents' permission. And I already have that," she laughed.

"Okay," he said.

He was wondering how he was going to manage that and she misinterpreted his look of concern.

"Oh, it wouldn't be that bad," she said gaily. "We could go to museums after school, or on Saturday. The Modern Museum's great. Have you been there?" He shook his head and she lit another cigarette. "You'd like it. Of course I'd be a drag but look at the wonderful art education you'd be getting. I know them all. Backwards. I practically live there."

"Okay. Some day," he said, liking the idea.

She leaned her head back and looked out the frosted plate glass window, far away for a moment. She had a nice profile, he thought. Even when her face was relaxed and she wasn't talking and being animated with that fire going inside her, she looked pretty.

"Maybe a movie sometime." She was back with him again. "Of course there's the problem of getting there. Not to mention leaving. But if sometime you happen not to be in a big hurry—with important things to do—"

"I got no place to go," he said.

She put out her cigarette and flicked a bit of paper from her lower lip. Then she snapped her bag shut and adjusted her coat collar. "I decided to let you pay," she said, looking at him levelly. "For the treat of being with me."

He wanted to tell her that it really *was* a treat, that he couldn't remember when he'd ever had a more pleasant time.

Come on, you dummy, speak up! he told himself.

But I can't. I've been a dummy too long.

Okay, you dummy.

He took his hand out of his pocket and there was a dollar bill there. He put it on the table. The check read eighty cents. Lucky he had enough on him, he thought. Maybe he'd get another letter from his father in a day or so. *So what if I don't? So I just won't eat another of those rotten school hamburgers. Big deal.*

Then she was looking intently at him and he felt a flush reddening his face. Did she guess that was all he had?

Instead she said, "It's funny but I know I've seen you someplace. You look awfully familiar. Is your face always mad?"

"I guess so," he said, wondering where she possibly could have seen him. In the lobby of their building? That was possible, although he was certain that he'd never set eyes on her before. Then, as he regarded her wan heart-shaped face and pale yellow hair, something clicked inside him.

"Why are you smiling?" she asked.

"Because we've already met," he said. And when she shook her head, sending her hair flying, he added, "You've got a black telescope."

Deep inside, he had a chilled feeling. *I sure hope you're right this time. We goofed on this one once before. What is it? some kind of sickness with you about blond girls and telescopes? Maybe you oughtta see a doctor, only this time about your head.*

He looked directly at her and for a second he couldn't tell. Her mouth popped open. Her eyes widened. He could swear she was thinking about it. That was odd, he thought. You ought to know about something like that: you either have a black telescope or you don't. Or else you have one of another color. Or you don't.

She pointed her finger at him and jabbed it in the air. "I got it!" she said triumphantly. "You're eighteenth floor terrace. South wing! *My building!*" Then she clapped her hands to her face, lost in laughter.

He had to marvel at how easily she laughed. And there was nothing of contriteness or apology about her. He remembered the rages he'd gone into because he didn't know who the mysterious "peeper" was. Now he knew and he felt sheepish. *If I was a cripple and couldn't get out much, maybe I'd want to spend my time that way looking at people, too. Just to see what's going on in the world.*

Her fit of laughter finally subsided and she dabbed at her eyes with a small handkerchief having colored flowered corners. "Well, I was right," she gasped. "I *did* see you someplace. And you certainly *were* mad!"

A grin found his face and stayed. He didn't say anything. He just sat there grinning at her happily.

She put on her heavy blue coat with the red pile lining and flipped the peppermint scarf around her neck carelessly.

"Now that I've found out, there's nothing left to say," she said, sliding off the seat and moving her hands along the table to balance herself. "But don't worry," she added, "I'll think of something."

"It's okay," he said, following her, hesitant about offering his arm. He knew how proud she was. "It's just that I don't like being looked at. Like in talking, too. I don't talk much because of this dumb lisp. That's why I sound like such a dummy."

"I didn't notice," she said, as they got outside. "Anyway, at our age, girls are supposed to be brighter than boys. It's a simple biological fact. I think," she added.

"How come?" he asked.

"We mature earlier."

I guess that's possible, he thought as he walked her across the street. *Anyway, what do I know about it?*

She took his arm and he tried to walk as slowly as

he could, pretending he didn't feel the cold wind biting at his bones.

No doorman waited to churn the big glass revolving doors at this end of their building, which was fortunate, because Roger knew even he had to be fast and ready to hop every time they spun around. He opened the alternate side door and she went through without any trouble.

The lobby was deserted. There was no elevator man on this side, either. Roger stomped his feet, knocking off the snow, making believe he didn't want to track any snow into the building but really trying to get warm.

She pressed the black button for the elevator and said, "You know, you ought to get some warmer clothing for this kind of weather."

He wondered if she'd guessed. Then, pointing at her red and white long woolly scarf, he told her he intended getting one of those things, too.

"You mean my scarf?"

He nodded. Then she was uncurling it in a quick sweeping movement and to his great surprise handing it to him. He backed off a step.

"Go on, don't be silly. Take it," she said.

Unable to speak, he just waved his hands to let her know he couldn't take it.

She said, "I've got hundreds of them. Go ahead. Take it."

"Well, okay," he said, holding it in his hands.

The automatic elevator car came down and the doors bumped open but she just said, "Let's see how you look," and took the scarf out of his unresisting hand. She flung it around his neck and caught it deftly on the other side, then sent it flying around again and did something to it. She patted the ends and took a step back. He stood there hardly breathing. She tilted her head back, then nodded with a satisfied tightening of her lips.

"Just perfect," she said. "You look great and now I won't have to worry about your catching pneumonia."

He looked down and saw the long, flapping, striped peppermint ends and grinned his pleasure. The scarf felt very warm, too. He wondered for a fleeting moment if there was any difference between the mufflers girls and boys wore. Maybe some bright person would catch the difference and laugh. *So if they want to laugh, let 'em. I couldn't care less. Who cares what those dopes think anyway.*

"Well," she said, "maybe you can stop grinning and say good-by."

But he just stood there flat-footed, looking down at the red and white scarf, and the grin stayed. He looked up and into her eyes and it still wouldn't go away.

"It's not a million dollars," she reminded him. "It's only my red and white scarf."

I know, he wanted to say, *but I sure like it a lot. Say something, dummy!*

But again he wasn't able to.

She let out an exaggerated sigh, shrugged her blue-clad shoulders and waved her hands expressively. Then she was in the car, and he still stood there, helplessly wearing the crooked grin.

"You mean you're actually not going to say anything? You're just going to stand there with that grin?"

He could only nod his head, and the smile was definitely a part of his face now and wouldn't go away.

"All right," she said lightly. "Remind me not to ever give you anything again."

She didn't wave good-by. She merely moved her fingers in a little trilling gesture. Then without taking her eyes off him, she jabbed sideways at a button on the wall of the car and he heard the soft whooshing sounds of the doors closing between them, then the elevator going up. He watched the red eye of the indicator glow until her car stopped and the red light faded off.

After a while he turned and walked on the rubberized mat along the empty lobby to the other side of the building. There were nicely contoured chairs and couches and marble-topped tables with bright lamps on them running along the walls, and mirrors extending almost the whole length of the building without a break in their glittering line.

As he passed the mirrors, he nearly didn't recognize himself wearing the long bright red-and-white wool scarf and the crooked grin.

CHAPTER FOURTEEN

NATURALLY She wanted him to take off the bright woolly scarf when he got inside upstairs but he wouldn't. She didn't make too much of a fuss. She had a dinner appointment—and theater too, She told him—and was fixing Herself up after the beauty parlor. She only asked him where he got that outlandish-looking thing.

He recognized the signs that told him She was too busy now to really go into it. He mumbled something from another room. He knew She was too distracted to pin him down and ask what was that again.

When Her date came, She called to Roger and he came out of his room to meet the man, still wearing the muffler around his neck. She shot him an annoyed look but that was all and he guessed She didn't want to get mad and mean in front of Her new date.

"This is Mr. Miguel Hernandez, Roger. He's a bullfighter down in Mexico City."

"Matador," the slim olive-skinned man said, partly for her benefit, partly for Roger's, and bowed slightly. Roger shook the extended hand and was surprised to find it leathery. The man was dressed so well, in neat dark expensive-looking clothes, that he expected somehow his hands would be pale and soft. Only they weren't. How could you get such tough hands with all those calluses from fighting bulls?

"Do you kill them?" Roger asked.

The man nodded, "Si." His teeth were large and very even and white. They looked strong. But you needed more than strong teeth to fight a bull, Roger knew. You needed a sword, too, and he wondered how that felt.

"You have to kill them," the man was saying. "If you do not, he is only suffering too much and the people, the spectators, do not like that."

His voice was liquid and smooth and he moved the same way, in a flowing motion, catlike and indolently, but very straight and well-balanced. He wore his dark shining hair long, almost full at the back of his neck, the same way the kids wore it, and long and full at the sides. His shoulders were carried high and square and even though he moved like a dancer Roger had once seen, a Spanish one too, he looked very tough and athletic. His face was tough, too, his eyes hard and glittering, his cheekbones high and jutting like an Indian's.

He looked like a man who could stand up to danger, Roger thought. Behind the man's polite manner, he could sense something savage. Perhaps it was the dark glitter in his eyes or the way his wide mouth was set.

Maybe you've got to look like that to fight bulls, he thought. Maybe the bulls know it, too. That they've got a man in front of them they've got to look out for. That they've either got to kill him, hook him with those sharp thrusting horns, or else.

He wondered briefly how his mother got to meet a man like this dangerous-looking matador.

She was wearing something long and tight and shimmering that he had never seen before, and a dark blue velvet-looking evening coat. She had Her hair piled up on top of her head like a movie star. She looked pretty, he had to admit that.

She reached over to pat his face but he drew back, and her hand with the white scented glove seemed to hang frozen in the air for a second before She let it fall to her side. She didn't bat Her eyes but he saw a slight thin frowning line between them.

"Don't stay up too late now, Roger," She said.

"What time will you be home?" he asked.

"Late," She said, and turned to go.

The matador saluted him with his leathery hand.

"*Buenas noches,*" he said softly, showing his strong white teeth. Then in one long swinging step, he was at the white foyer door and had it open. She swept out, his dark form followed, and the door closed with a soft click.

Roger was alone.

He looked down at the long red and white flapping ends of the scarf Nemo Newman had given him. He unwound it from his neck very carefully, so as not to forget how she had done it. He held it now near the center, his hands far apart. Suddenly extending his arms, he sent the ends flapping out and then snapped them sharply.

"Hey, *toro!*" he said, remembering the way he had seen it done in movies and on TV. He took another step forward and flapped it again. "Ah, *toro,*" he said between clenched teeth. The bull was waiting somewhere beyond the circle of light, in the darkness near the windows. He stamped his heels quickly and snapped the scarf-ends out again. Then it was coming. It came on thunderous hooves in a swift straight line right at him. At the last possible second, when the horns were almost upon him, when he could almost smell the bull's hot breath, he pivoted, drawing his left foot back, dropping the red scarf close to his sides. He made himself as thin as possible, holding his breath. The bull passed, and looking down he saw he was untouched. *Whew! That was close,* he told himself.

He could imagine the roar of the crowd and then he had to pull himself together and prepare for the next charge of the snorting, pawing dark shape out there. He lifted the long woolly scarf again and flapped out the red and white ends.

"Hey, *toro!* Ah-h-h, *toro,*" he crooned, advancing his feet in a crabwise movement. He took three steps, flapping the scarf-ends out toward the pawing figure with each one. Then he heard it coming. He placed his hands to the right side now, intending to bring the bull that way. It was more difficult for him that way; somehow he felt more natural when he brought the bull in on his left. But he knew he had to show them that he could dominate the bull from all sides. So he waited now, flicking it again in a taunting motion, and then it loomed up suddenly dark and fearsome in its hairy black bulk and he saw briefly the raw bloody patches where the *banderillas* had been planted. His concentration was broken by the blood —how much blood had the brave animal lost already? —and then it was upon him and although he had his hands back toward his right hip now, somehow he did not have them out quite far enough.

He saw dimly, too late, the swerving dipping movement of the big red-eyed head (he'd forgotten this one hooked to the right) and then the hard sharp prong of the horn was in him and he felt himself pierced with the agonizing sudden thrust. Then he was lifted on the powerful neck and thrown high in the air. He fell and was still.

He couldn't get up. The pain was too much. Then he heard the sound of the thudding hooves again and he knew he had to do something or he would be gored, perhaps horribly maimed. *Get up, you dummy!* he screamed silently to himself, realizing almost instantly that he shouldn't humiliate himself that way, not when he was a famous matador. He got to one knee, holding his groin, trying to stop the spurting blood that was draining his insides. He could hardly stand the pain but he knew he had to do something. The bull was charging and he knew he didn't have a second to lose.

It's easy, he tried to tell himself. *All you've got to do is grab your sword and you can still get out of this alive.* He looked down at his other hand and there was no sword there, only the limp end of the bloody scarf.

What am I supposed to do now, stab him with this?

The noise of the bull came closer and he heard the crowd screaming. He would have to stay there and take it. The screaming shrilled louder in his ears and he turned his head to tell them there was nothing he could do, and then he understood it was the telephone ringing. He crawled over to it, holding his side, careful not to get any blood on Her carpet.

"I was just wondering if you could talk yet," Nemo Newman said in his ear. "Or are you still grinning in ecstasy?"

"Oh, hi!" he said.

He rolled over on the rug to get comfortable, and as he put his hand up behind his head he noticed there was no blood there. He sighed with relief, shivering with a sudden chill and wondering if the matador who had gone out with his mother had ever been gored. *I guess he must have been,* he told himself. *They all are, you know, sooner or later.*

"Come on, talk," Nemo Newman yelled. "I can't use the telescope on you any more so I have to use the phone. Now it's your turn to say something. And hurry up! I have to be in bed by midnight."

He had to shake his head and smile, wondering how she had found out his telephone number. *Well, it's easy enough, dummy. All you probably do is ask information. The only difference is she used her head and found out. You didn't, period.*

He didn't tell her how handy the red scarf was for

bull fighting but he managed to think of something to say: how great it was having coffee together, and all, and that he'd like to go to that Museum of Modern Art with her some time, a movie too, if he could get out at night.

Later, lying in bed, he still wore the scarf. She sure had a lot of personality, he thought. She was the first one in New York, now that he thought about it, to call him on the phone. *And you didn't even thank her for the scarf, lunkhead!*

Feeling its warmth, he thought he really should have said something. And then he was remembering another time when he should have said something. Thanks, at least. It didn't hurt to say thanks. . . .

He was holding the book about pirates that he'd wanted for such a long time, flipping the pages, looking at the exciting pictures, and then he saw Her feet still there, not moving, and he heard Her voice.

Say, thanks, Roger, and he realized suddenly Her voice was angry. He couldn't understand why She was so angry when he was so happy.

Can you hear me, Roger? Say thanks, I said, and Her voice was flat with insistence.

He was looking at a page where the pirates were all over the page, swinging from the ropes on to the other ship they had lashed somehow to their side. Some had long knives in their teeth. They had funny hats on the long boots and ragged trousers. Soldiers below were firing at them led by one tall straight man with a mustache.

*All right, Roger, if you won't say thanks, then
I'll just have to take it away. You've got to
learn good manners.*

He couldn't believe it when Her hand was
there and he heard himself shrilling, *Okay, Okay,
so take it away, who cares, who wants this dumb
book anyway....*

He made himself get up now, out of bed. The heat
was turned off in the big building after nine, and the
rooms were chilly, but the lights were on all over, the
way he had left them. They still hadn't come home
yet. He realized how much colder he'd be without
the scarf, even in his own apartment, and he picked
up the phone and asked information if she could give
him Nemo Newman's phone number, and she told
him to wait just a moment, please. There was no
Nemo Newman at that address, she said, and he realized he'd given the same address as his instead of the
87th Street side. He waited while she went through
her list there and then she was telling him in a nice
regretful voice that there was no Nemo Newman
listed at that address, either. That flustered him and
he told her thanks, anyway, and hung up. He sat
brooding for a minute.

He got out their New York City directory and
started looking for the N's. As he turned the pages, he
suddenly knew what was wrong. It's got to be under
the name of her mother or father or whoever's there
to pay the bills.

He finally found it. There were a lot of Newmans
but only one at that exact address: Julius J. Newman,

it said, in small type. He wrote the number down but then was afraid to call, wondering who might answer it. *The trouble is, you just got no will power,* he told himself as he went back to bed.

He couldn't sleep. So much had happened to him on this day, good and bad. Was every day going to be like this one, filled with the shocks and disappointments of living, an occasional good thing thrown in, like a peace offering or a piece of candy?

Maybe Pop goes through days like this, he thought. *That's why he's always looking so worried. He's always got that pressure, knowing somehow that something is going to be fouled up and he's going to get a panning in the "trades."* Those little papers that all the show-business people read all the time and threw down so angrily sure must be important. There were two of them, dailies, about the size of a small magazine, containing only six to ten pages. One had its masthead trimmed in red ink, the other used green. . . .

His father held the green one in his hand, his mouth drawn back in a bitter line and Roger could see his hand shaking when he said, "They can kill you here. One lousy review!"

It was a picture he had done on a small budget, to please the studio heads, and everything possible had gone wrong on location.

The leading ladies didn't get along and one left the set in tears and didn't come back. They had to get another one in a hurry and the male star wasn't too happy about that because he liked the first one. So he loafed through his part and didn't give a good performance. The director couldn't do anything because the star was a bigger name than he was. Finally he quit and an assistant director took over. He let everybody have their own way to get the picture finished on time and naturally it turned out bad. When the Name writer saw what they had done to his script he insisted they remove his name from the screen credits. And the movie critics in Hollywood who knew something of the inside story blasted the picture. The only one left important enough to blame was Roger's father.

"So they panned him," he heard his mother say over the phone that same day, "and he's taking it hard. I can't understand why. It was an awful piece of junk to begin with. He dragged me to their sneak preview, and if we hadn't had a party of our own guests along, I would have walked out in ten minutes."

So you didn't have to be in the bull ring to get killed, he thought now. He knew too well how hard his father worked every day and he wondered now, as he remembered seeing him always harried and withdrawn as he tried to concentrate on his problems, if he got "killed" that way every day.

How often did the matador fight? Every day? Once a week? If you killed a bull one day, could you kill one the next? And then another one after that? *Maybe* he *could*, he thought. *Not me.*

Then he remembered hearing or reading—he wasn't sure which—that sometimes the famous ones got to fight as many as five bulls a day. Fighting five means killing five, he thought. They're not out there just for the exercise. Maybe they get paid more for each one and that's why they like to put in a full day like that.

It's crazy. Here I can't even sleep without doing anything to anybody. How would it be if I just finished killing five bulls?

He shook his head. *To tell the truth, I don't think I could kill even one. I guess maybe you've got to have the killer instinct for that.* He saw in his mind's eye the wide cruel mouth and the eyes that glittered, the lithe catlike stride, and felt again the hidden savagery behind the mask of the polite, soft-spoken, very well-groomed matador, Hernandez.

I'd like to see those Greenwich Village kids start up with him! Come to think of it, they wouldn't be chasing him, either. Not that guy.

And not that Roger Tunnell either; not unless they were tired of living.

How would his father do with those Village toughs? He's out of shape; besides, he's a business man. They can't fight.

I wonder what he's doing now? Missing me? Oh, sure! That's all he has on his mind. He probably doesn't even know I'm gone.

He didn't remember getting up but he was in the living room, sitting on the couch and looking down at the white telephone in his hand. Now how did that get there? he wondered. Then he heard the clicks and whirrs and soft chimes and beeps.

I hope he's still there; it's only nine o'clock here so

he ought to still be there. Maybe I can do it again for him. I said Rolls Royce today and Jerry Jeeks. I ought to be able to say my own name when the time comes.

Yeah, you sure ought to. What's that name again?

"Roger," he said. "Then there's rain and ripples and rugs and carpets. There's—dingdong—a river and a—gr-rr—bird and a—a—"

Okay, that's enough already, he told himself. *Don't waste it. Save it.*

Then he heard the phone ringing and his father's voice say, "Hello."

"This is Roger," he said, and added, "with a capital R."

You did it, you did it! he almost screamed to himself.

"Hello, hello," he heard his father saying. "Who is this?"

Oh, heck, he thought despairingly, *he didn't hear. Can we do it again? That was such a good one. Yeah, it sure was but don't cry, don't get excited. That's bad for you. Remember what she said. Just drop the jaw. Ahh——like that, attaboy. Now come on, growl, growl—grr-rr—grrr—*

"Hello," his father was saying, "will you please speak up? I can't hear you."

"Gr—rrr," he said. "It's Roger, Pop. Your son from New York." He took a deep breath and shut his eyes and said, "Roger."

"Roger?" he heard his father say, surprised. "Is that you calling, Roger?"

"Yeah, Pop. It's me, all right. All *right*," he repeated.

"Well, this is a nice surprise. How are you, son?"

"I'm fine. Did you notice I could say my name?"

"What's that?"

"I said I could say my name."

"Of course you can, son. How's your mother?"

He didn't hear me, he didn't hear what I did, I did all those lousy AH's perfect and he didn't even hear 'em.

"Speak up, son. Stop mumbling. I can hardly hear you."

"Yeah, I know," he said.

"I asked you, how is your mother?"

"She's fine. She just went out with a bull fight-uh."

"What? Did you say a bullfighter?"

"Yeah."

"Now, son, will you please settle down and stop talking nonsense. I asked you—"

"A *bull* fight-uh. A *bull* fight-uh," he yelled. "Don't you get it?" He made a sound of a bull but it seemed to come out more like a cow mooing.

"Roger, will you please stop making those silly animal sounds? I thought you were all over that. Now I'd like to talk to you but I have some important people over here now for a story conference and if you can't—"

He made the sound of the morning rooster then and his eyes were blurry but he found the long telephone cord where it went into the metal box on the wall, and he yanked as hard as he could. It came out of the metal box easily.

He sat down on the couch again, holding the phone, the broken disconnected wire, and he spoke into the dead receiver.

"I could have spelled it for you, too," he said. "Just listen to what you missed. Capital R – O – G – E – R." He threw the phone on the floor and it bumped across the rug.

Well, what did you expect, big brain? He never did listen.

CHAPTER FIFTEEN

HE LEFT the apartment early the next morning without bothering to wake Her for his lunch money.

So I won't eat. Big deal!

The telephone had been put back on the low cocktail table so he knew She'd noticed it, all right.

Well, I guess we'll hear about that later. But don't let's worry about that now. We got enough right now to keep us going until then.

The snow was almost gone from the streets. All that remained were dribbles of gray, dissolving in the black soot and grime of the city. "Oh, that's just great," he murmured. "All it looks like now is a bunch of slop."

He had enough fare for his school bus. He sat in the back completely depressed, paying no attention to the other children, keeping his face pressed hard against the cold glass windowpane.

"I got some important people here—" he said aloud

in a low mocking voice. "Big deal. He's always got important people waiting. Me and my bright ideas."

Come to think of it, that was only part of how dumb you are. You forgot to make that call collect! That means She's going to get the bill and that'll give Her another reason for kissing you. You can guess what She'll tell you, can't you?

"It's perfectly all right for you to call your father if you wish. But he's very rich and can afford the long distance call. We can't. Do you realize what we could buy for the price of your stupid unnecessary telephone call?"

No. Tell me. Tell me. Maybe one treatment at the beauty parlor, so we could have our hair all fixed up nice and pretty for the bullfighter?

Maybe an overcoat for your loving son?

Okay. I know that's ridiculous. How about boots? They're pretty cheap, aren't they? Or even a scarf, a muffler, so people won't have to take pity on me and give me theirs—people who are always falling down because they can't walk straight and don't want to let you help them up when they do.

He wondered if Nemo Newman was going to have any trouble walking to school today. His spear-eyed glance roved the streets speculatively. No ice. So maybe she'll make it okay today.

He dragged his feet up the wet slush of the school steps and headed reluctantly for his Home Room and his morning encounter with Mr. Rawling. As he rounded the corridor corner, he saw the door open as usual, and skulking almost furtively outside it the tall stooped figure of Dudley Appleton.

Well, he made it on time today! Maybe they fired the chauffeur or got a new Rolls. Anyway, what's he doing out here when he can get himself in good by reporting early? Appleton turned and saw him, and heaved a big sigh of relief. He put out his hand as if to stop Roger, then smiled nervously and gulped, his face reddening.

"I w-want to t-thank you for—for y-yesterday," he said. "It was m-m-mighty nice of y-you, B-B-Baxter."

He's stammering, the dope! I knew they were getting to him. Well, like I guessed, Miss Clemm's going to have another customer.

He avoided Appleton's hand. Then, in a cold detached tired voice that surprised him, he said, "Fuh what?" and walked past Appleton as if he weren't there. He reached his seat and sat down, feeling cold and tired. He saw Mr. Rawling sitting at the desk and pretended that he didn't.

Attendance was better this day, the classroom as full as he could ever remember. He began to feel warm and perspire, and then he became aware of whispering behind him. It picked up and ran to the sides. He turned his head and saw them all looking at him, smiling a strange kind of smile that he couldn't understand. Then he got it. They were all looking at the long red-and-white wool scarf he was still wearing and 'had forgotten for the moment. His hand moved involuntarily toward it, then he forced his hand down. He looked back at them without expression.

Drop dead, he told them all silently.

Mr. Rawling surveyed the class, flicked his eyes

once in Roger's direction and back again to the class. The murmuring stopped.

It's okay, Don't worry, he noticed. He's not saying anything now but don't hold your breath. When he's good and ready you'll get the snapper. Meanwhile, he's letting it build up. I'm just telling you all this so you won't be surprised later.

Yeah, thanks a lot.

Mr. Rawling surprised him by not calling the roll. "Well, I see you're all here this morning so we can dispense with the formalities."

He saw Appleton there, too. *What's wrong?* Roger wondered. *No cracks about the chauffeur or the car today? Maybe he's sick.*

He looked sharply at Mr. Rawling and had to admit the teacher never looked healthier. Every strand of hair was in place, rich and glowing, his fair complexion radiated good health and he sat without the slightest stoop or slouch in a pink shirt with green tie and brown sports jacket over gray trousers.

"I'd like to suggest a few books for all you illiterates out there," he said, with a good-humored smile. "I assume some of you are acquainted with what books are"—he made an explanatory motion with his well-shaped hands—"those little things with a lot of paper and type between hard covers. Sometimes, paper covers."

Roger wrote the titles and authors down, surprised to notice that he had read them all. Mr. Rawling merely gave questioners in the class a mute look of surprise and then, without grandstanding, spelled out the troublesome titles and names.

It was a nice friendly easy-going relaxed session and Roger, very warm in his tight scarf, was dumbfounded. The bell rang and he rose with the others to leave.

Mr. Rawling's soft drawling voice seemed to sink right into his back. "Oh, Baxter, would you mind stopping here for a moment? I won't keep you long."

Well, I told you. I told you it wouldn't last, right? Didn't I?

Aw, sheddup! he answered himself.

He walked back, keeping himself straight, not dawdling, his expression blank. A few in the class, sensing something in the making, loitered to look aimlessly about for things while they kept their eyes on the teacher and Roger. Mr. Rawling dismissed them with a brisk contempt.

"You are all excused," he told them, his manicured hand pointing eloquently toward the door, and they giggled guiltily, a few primped, and then they all walked slowly toward the open door.

Roger stood holding his books low in his hands, not leaning against the convenient blackboard, until the last of them had gone. Marion Johnson had made a slight movement with her hand as she passed, crossing her fingers.

Thanks a lot, he thought. *I guess I'll need it.*

He told himself silently, *Now don't be nervous. It'll be over in a little while, take my word for it. It can't be as bad as being alone in that bullring waiting for the bull to come at you. He does it all the time. That Miguel Hernandez. Do you think he's nervous?*

What kind of a question is that? How do I know if he's nervous?

Okay, okay. So you don't know. Don't get excited. That's bad for you. All I was asking was, all I meant was, do you think you'd be nervous?

Well, to tell you the truth, I guess so, but I don't know. Put it down, it's some more I don't know.

If it was life or death, you'd be nervous. If it had to be your life or his, you'd be. Who you kidding?

I tell you I don't know, and if you're going to worry about that, who told you to take that creepy kind of job in the first place? As a matter of fact, if you really want to know something, right now not only don't I feel nervous, I don't feel anything.

He waited for the stragglers to leave and wondered why he wasn't nervous.

Funny. I ought to be. This must be a serious situation but it's like I got no feelings, all of a sudden. The only feeling I got is that I'm empty and I'm numb all over, which isn't the same. It's more like I died or something.

Can you die standing up? He pinched himself to make sure. He felt merely the lightest sensation in his thigh, where he had nipped the flesh hard between his thumb and forefinger.

Well, I felt something, so I guess I'm living. Only I thought I pinched hard enough to hurt.

Okay, okay. Maybe that proves you're getting tougher. Maybe you're developing a thicker skin.

His eyes saw the last of them pull the door shut behind him. He saw Mr. Rawling's eyes swing in his direction.

Well, right now the way you feel, you don't care.

It's like you're getting pretty far away from it and he won't be able to reach you.

I think it's something like that. I just hope I can stay out here where he can't reach me. Then I won't lose my temper and say or do something I'll have to be sorry for after.

Like that time with the TV set, he reminded himself.

His eyes, wide open, saw Mr. Rawling take a step toward the door and lean up to look out the glass part of it and then he didn't see him any more. His mind was leading him back to another room, large and very bright with sunshine. He could see the tall fan palms alternating like steps towering over the queen palms out on the street.

That looks like Beverly Hills. I know that room. Hey, is that me in that room? I sure was small and skinny then, wasn't I? I guess it was a long time ago. . . .

The short plump man with the bushy black beard sat at his desk, holding a long dark cigar. Dr. Gottering, the head shrinker. The noted child psychologist. At least, that's what They told everybody he was. Well, it cost them a lot of money but now they knew for sure their son Roger was hostile.

Dr. Gottering was asking why the small skinny kid put his foot through the damn TV set.

The kid said because he couldn't stand that jerk of a Jerry Jeeks—because everybody seemed to love him and they all laughed and he was getting ten thousand dollars a week for it.

And was that why he hated him?

No, it was because he got hit and punished for talking the same way and doing the same dumb things.

That made the doctor blink all right. . . .

Roger's eyes flickered, his thoughts wavered. Now, again, he saw Mr. Rawling framing a slight tentative smile between his lips. He seemed to be saying the same words over again. "—Miss Clemm has told me a little about your history and I want you to know that I'm fully aware—"

What's he saying? he thought. Then, although he kept looking straight at Mr. Rawling, noticing the hurt look in his eyes, his own mind was taking him back to that other room. *Just hold it a minute, will you, please?* he wanted to tell Mr. Rawling. *This is important. I see some other people there. Yeah, it must have been pretty important because there we all are, together for a change. . . .*

"Now, if you haff any questions—" Dr. Hermann Gottering was saying, with his funny accent. This time the little man with the beard was wearing a light striped vest inside his dark coat, but still taking three puffs of his cigar after each sentence he spoke, then putting the cigar down carefully in a large blue ash tray on the desk, folding his soft white hands together.

"How come you got a beard?" Roger heard himself ask.

Before the little man could answer, the father interrupted almost savagely. "So he can charge fifty dollars a visit, instead of the twenty-five everybody else in town is getting."

The doctor laughed pleasantly.

Mr. Rawling's face suddenly got in the way and even though he was speaking in a very low voice, Roger couldn't hear what the doctor was saying. *Oh, come on,* he wanted to tell Mr. Rawling, *have a heart. Didn't I ask you to please wait?*

"—because you're new here, you're not yet oriented to my style—" Then Mr. Rawling's voice faded in spots at first, and the light in the room seemed to flicker. "—the level of comprehension here—a bunch of rich kids here, after all it's a private school, and they're spoiled rotten—lazy, self-indulgent—and as a teacher, I had to find a way of reaching them—and possibly in your anxiety—"

Roger saw the long cigar go down in the blue ash tray and the wreath of smoke over the doctor's face as he folded his hands and told Roger's father and mother, "Would you believe a compulsion neurosis stemming from a long-existing anxiety state?"

His father exploded. "Good Lord! Everybody is a comic these days!"

Why was his father getting so mad? The

"would you believe?" expression had been made popular by a TV comic, and had become the thing to say.

Even the Japanese gardener, when Roger asked him the name of the plant he was putting in the soft ground near the yew, said without a moment's pause: "Rood you bereeve Abyssinian banana tree?"

Gottering was still sitting there, his belly moving up and down as he laughed, his vest moving with it. Then he stopped laughing. "This boy is suffering from the condition, not too unusual today, of haffing two highly intelligent, busily preoccupied, unconditionally detached people for parents."

Then he picked up his cigar. There was a long ash at the end of it and he handled the cigar very carefully, as if it were hot. He held it out in front of him until Roger's father had to focus his eyes on it. Then Gottering made an abrupt movement with his hand and the ash fell from the cigar and spattered on the clean shining surface of his big desk.

"You haff to be careful how you handle even a cigar, my friends," he said.

Mr. Baxter didn't look sympathetic. His mouth lines were drawn back and bitter. "Listen, Gottering, for what you charge, you can shake your hand all day and smoke all you want of them."

The plump man nodded as if in agreement. "Yes. I can use them up fast and throw them away. But if you handle a cigar carefully, so the ash doesn't fall, it smokes sweeter."

Then his father said, "Yeah. I suppose so. But I'm here to talk about the kid, not about your cigars."

The doctor spoke as if to his cigar, moodily. "Out here, people don't listen. You talk but they don't listen. They just vant something done."

He didn't pick up the cigar this time and put it in his mouth for his customary three puffs. He just held it there, staring at it and shaking his head.

Now Mr. Rawling was shaking his head. The roaring in Roger's ears subsided and he could see Mr. Rawling more clearly now. He looked out the window for the incredibly tall, slender, curving, clump-topped fan palms but all he saw was the dull leaden New York City sky and then some snow on an adjacent building top.

Mr. Rawling was saying, "—you made a judgment without understanding. It means my prodding them, sticking them, flaying a little skin now and then."

He looks different somehow, Roger thought. He isn't acting cute now.

Mr. Rawling was continuing, "—naturally with your background and intelligence you would react this way, but if you would realize you're like an outsider judging us—you came into class so late—and an outsider can't see we're just a big happy family. All he observes is the wrangling. But there's love there, too, although you can't see it—"

Roger blinked. He noticed Mr. Rawling's face was pale with patches of color near his cheekbones. He doesn't have high cheekbones, he thought, and wondered if he, himself, ever would. He had forgotten for the moment what his own face looked like and he wanted to feel his cheekbones to find out if they were prominent or not, but he decided not to. His eyes quartered the room and he saw it was empty. *Hey, it looks like everybody's gone. What am I doing here? I guess I better get out. I'm probably late for—what?* he wondered, and wasn't able to think of what he might be late for.

He started to walk for the door and then he saw Mr. Rawling standing in his way. His face was very tense and earnest and it appeared to be talking to him.

I guess he wants to tell me something, but I don't think I can wait because I'm late for someplace.

He could make out some of Mr. Rawling's words but they seemed to be about love and understanding and that didn't make sense to him.

I guess he's practicing a speech or something for the English class. I better get out before he asks me what I'm doing here. I better get out of here and go someplace.

Then he walked out of the room and he thought he heard Mr. Rawling say, "Well, good-by for now, Roger, and thank you."

CHAPTER SIXTEEN

HE HAPPENED to look up at the large school clock high on the corridor wall and he saw the hand pointing to five minutes past the hour.

Oh, great! Now I lost five minutes someplace. I got to get more on the ball so I don't lose so much time between classes.

He felt very tired, his books heavy in his arms. *I got to put these down someplace. These books are awfully heavy.*

Then he heard the sound of footsteps walking along the hallway. *That's funny; there's nobody walking here but me. How can I hear footsteps?* Then he traced the sound and saw the footsteps were his. He watched the way his feet moved, pleased to see the toes of his wet shoes moving straight ahead, pointing parallel to each other, not straying over to an oblique angle but always straight ahead, dead parallel. *Hey, that's neat!* But he didn't know why he liked it. *I guess Indians used to walk that way,* he thought, *until they became poor and drunk in Palm Springs.*

He looked up at the clock again, worried in case he might have lost too much time admiring the movement of his feet. This time he couldn't see any numerals on it. *That's okay, don't worry about it. They always tell you how late you are.*

Now he noticed the swaying ends of his long scarf and liked the rhythm of their responding with an alternate swinging motion to his own stride. He made himself stop abruptly and lean over to watch. The ends kept moving, flipping almost defiantly a few more times before coming to rest.

It's like they got a mind of their own, he marveled.

He walked along the left side of the corridor for a while, edging his feet along the baseboard crabwise, one sliding step forward following the other. Then he got tired of that and tried the other side. This time he spun out and couldn't make his feet remain in contact with the black baseboard trim. *Next time I fight a bull, I got to remember that that's my weak side. That's how he got me the other time.*

He was very tired now. And then he came to a door that looked familiar. There were black letters on a white card in a thin black frame that said: SPEECH CLINIC. *I'm sorry, Jack,* he told himself, *but I'm dropping out of this race. I'm real beat and they got some nice soft chairs in here.*

The door opened easily without any squeaks, and it made a soft hissing sound behind him when it closed, then a little soft click. He thought he heard the sounds but wasn't sure where they came from. He no-

ticed a large bulky woman sitting with a desk in front
of her, her face very quiet-looking and her chin thrust
out like a bulldog's. He thought she looked at him in
a nice polite interested way as he walked across the
carpet to the green leather chair near the wall. The
heavy books slid away from his hands.

"I need a lot of sleep," he told her, "so don't let
me bother you."

He curled his body in the chair like an animal,
covering his dark tousled hair with his arms. Then he
remembered something, straightened up, flicked his
eyes open and found hers, and said: "Just don't let
me get too loose, that's all." He closed his eyes and
then opened them again to add, "*Por favor*. That's
Mexican. It means *please*," he explained.

He slept curled up that way for five minutes and
then he was awake again. He saw the bulky woman
still at the desk where the light was and then he felt
something soft and warm on him. He wasn't sure what
it was but it could be a blanket. He searched for his
chest and tapped it, then found his knees and tapped
them. Then he put his hands under the blanket and
did the same thing.

"Well, I guess we're still here," he said and then
was asleep again.

When his eyes flicked open again they swept toward the woman at the desk and his hands repeated
their search over his body. He nodded as if satisfied
and slept again. He did this twice more in the next
ten minutes. Then he sat up, pushing the blanket
away from him.

"Hey, where'd this come from?" he asked and the

woman at the desk told him they kept things like that handy for friends. He nodded and felt it. Then he stroked his scarf and it seemed to him they felt almost the same.

The woman at the desk wasn't writing with her pen now. She was busy with something shining that looked like silver and there was a wreath of steam around it. She poured from this down into a big green mug on her desk. Then she asked him if he would like some tea and he couldn't make up his mind if he would or wouldn' t. She said it was a cold day, just the kind of a day for tea, and he didn't have any opinion about that either. She started to lift it across the desk toward him and then stopped her hand and asked if he wanted one lump or two. He said he didn't know and she dropped one lump in.

"You probably like cream in your tea," she said then, "and I'm sorry but I don't have any."

It didn't seem to make any difference to him but he said, "That's okay."

She passed the steaming mug to him and he saw a dark color inside but he didn't know what it was.

"I guess this is tea," he said and tasted it.

"I guess it is, too," she said. Then she asked him if he could guess her name and he thought about that for a while and then said he thought he could. Then he told her he wasn't sure.

"Don't rush me," he said. "This is hot." Then he asked her if there had been any calls for him and she didn't smile, and told him not a single one.

"This is a secret hideaway," she said. "Nobody knows we're living."

He put the mug down on the desk and touched his chest and legs again and made his feet wiggle and watched them. "Well, I'm glad to see I'm still here anyway," he said.

She asked him where he expected to be instead of there and he explained that he had the feeling he was going to disappear.

"Is that why you didn't want me to let you get too loose before?"

"I guess so," he said. His eyes roved the room again and fastened on the ceiling. "Hey, are we allowed to smoke in here?" he asked.

"I guess so," she said. "Why, do you smoke?"

"I don't know."

"How do you feel?" she asked.

"Feel? What's that?"

"Are you worried?"

"What does that mean—worried?" he said.

She took a white card out of her drawer and said, "You know, I don't believe I have your home phone number."

"That's okay," he said. Then, "if you want it, they'll give it to you."

"Who will?"

"The people there."

"Well, what if I want to call you some night when I'm home. You know, if I'm lonesome," she said.

He looked at her. "Don't you have a boy friend?"

"With this face?" she said, smiling.

He felt his own face. "Do I have any cheekbones?"

"Of course. Don't you feel them?"

He tapped his face. "I don't know. It's kinda hollow there."

She looked down at her card again. "You still didn't give me that phone number, you know, in case I want to call you."

"Didn't She tell you yet our phone isn't working?" She shook her head.

He shook his own head in imitation. "What does that mean?"

"Don't you know?"

"I guess so," he said. "But anyway it isn't working because I ripped it out last night. So save your money."

"I guess it was ringing too loud," Miss Clemm said.

"Nope," he said. "Wrong again." He reached for the mug and brought it to his lips. "My, this is good," he said. And then, "Do we always have to say that?"

"If you like to. And if you feel like saying it."

He nodded. "That's what I thought. I got another one fa you. Can you get *ah-wested* for what you think?"

"No," she said firmly. "Never. Otherwise I'd have been in jail for many many years."

"I didn't know about that," he said. "Anyway, so now I don't keh what I fink about that big fat dope."

"Which one is that?"

"You know. You know. That famous Hollywood big fat dope."

"Would that be your father?"

He bobbed his head several times. "You know what that dope did? I had my ah's all weddy for him last night. I could even tell him my own name. And you know what? He wouldn't even listen. He got mad because I was twying to tell him what the bullfighter sounded like."

"That's a shame, all right," she said. "But, don't worry. You'll get them back again. You've given me a lot of good R's today."

"I guess I can't depend on anything," he said. "I guess that's why I got this ulcer."

She looked mildly surprised. "Do you have an ulcer?"

"I pwobably got it fwom Huh wotten cooking." He prodded his stomach. "Can you feel an ulcer?"

"I don't think so," she said. "But, anyway, I'm not that kind of a doctor. I'm only one in speech therapy and psychology."

"That's pwobably why I got this empty feeling, Doc," he said, prodding and pushing his stomach. "Fwom eating all that wotten food and then having to throw it up." He gave his stomach a final tap. "It's no use, I guess. It looks like She made me use up my stomach."

"How could she do that?"

"Didn't I ever tell you?"

"If you did, I'm afraid I don't remember, Roger."

He scratched his head vigorously. "I think She was a bad girl. Can I tell you a secret?"

"Yes."

"Well, She used to save up all the food I didn't eat the whole week. And then one day, fuh a big suh-pwise, She would cook it up again and make me eat it. And

I would eat it but it was so wotten I hadda thwow it up—on the plate. And then—and then She would make me eat it up again—I mean—" he hesitated, "—*everything*. All that gook!" He looked at her appealingly. "Now that wasn't very nice, was it?" He pushed down on his stomach again. "No wonder I got no stomach. She made me use it all up."

Miss Clemm told him she agreed with him that it wasn't nice and her eyes were far away too. She asked him if he would mind if she examined his eyes and he said he didn't care. But when she looked in her desk drawer, she couldn't find something. He was twirling the end of his scarf again, making the colors spin, and she told him she admired his scarf. He bobbed his head several times and told her somebody had given it to him and when she asked who, he couldn't remember.

"It was gonna be part of my new life too," he said.

Then she put her telephone to her ear and said something and then put it down again. She got up from her chair and told him she had to get something from another office and asked him if he would please wait there, and he was bobbing his head. Please wait here, she told him, I'll be right back, and he kept bobbing his head and she left the room and closed the door quietly.

After a few minutes he looked up and there wasn't anybody in the room. *Come on,* he told himself, *you got a good rest and now you better get going so you won't be late. If you stay here you're liable to disappear and then she won't know where you are.*

He wanted to leave a note to thank the nice woman for the tea but he couldn't remember if he knew how to write. When he walked to the door he was holding his sides and he knew he was still there.

CHAPTER SEVENTEEN

NOBODY saw him leave Miss Clemm's room. He came to the front door of the school and he went out and down the still-wet steps and he kept on walking and soon he was far away.

He walked up Madison Avenue past the coffee shops and the music shops and the galleries and sweater shops for women. He turned east on 58th Street and kept walking until he saw the high arch and cables of the Queensboro Bridge. He crossed First Avenue and found himself at a dead end, a small cul-de-sac of a narrow street, where he leaned against a cold metal railing and looked down over the East River Drive at the passing tugs in the wide swirling river. He saw a small green island near the other side of the river with some red buildings filling most of it but he didn't know who lived there. He thought it was a funny place for that kind of building. *Gee, you can't even depend on an island.*

The wind was cool on his face. He threw his scarf ends over his shoulders and let the wind cool his body, too.

Behind a large red and white tug heading north pulling a garbage scow came a barge filled with ashes and another piled high with broken-down automobiles. The sun was bright in his eyes, reflecting burning shafts from the chrome and glass of the automobile scow, and at first he had the illusion they were shooting white arrows at him. *Come on*, he wanted to yell at them, *cut it out, I'm only a visitor*. But he didn't move and the scow shot its arrows farther up at the giant white building blocks lining the Drive. *That's better*, he told it, *that's more like it. Knock down the buildings if you want to, not me.*

He turned away and saw a nurse approaching, pushing a baby carriage. She wore a little white neatly folded perky kind of a cap, and a dark blue cape. Her skirt was white and so were her stockings and shoes. Her blond hair was cut short and made her look very young to be a nurse. He wondered if maybe the baby was sick and if he ought to take a look but decided he'd better not.

I'm not looking at any sick babies today.

The girl passed very close to him on the narrow walk. In turning slightly to give her more room he happened to look down and saw a baby with a very red face and large startling blue eyes giving him a big happy smile.

Roger said, "Lalala," the kind of sound he'd been meaning to make all day but hadn't, and the baby gurgled back at him waving its tiny fists, smiling its biggest smile. The girl wheeling the carriage smiled at Roger, too.

Well, that makes two happy faces for a change.

Suddenly it was as if an oppressive weight left him. He took a deep sighing breath and the air felt clean. He wanted to run after them and talk and play with the baby but guessed he'd better not. *I might give the kid my impediment. Or else she'll think I'm some kind of a nut and call a cop.*

He wheeled and ran criss-cross along the small dead-end street until he came to the corner. He saw the sign that said First Avenue and wondered how he had managed to cross before without seeing the red street light. *I guess I was walking in my sleep again.*

The street was very wide with one way traffic and when the light flashed green he was about to step off, but then he hesitated, wondering if that was the right color to cross on. He saw the cars waiting to move, and as long as they weren't moving he decided he'd better wait, too. Then the light flashed red and the cars moved quickly and he stepped off the curb and nearly got knocked down by a car.

"Watch the light, stupid," a man yelled from inside.

But I did, he wanted to say.

A fat Negro woman came out of a laundry shop on the corner carrying a large wicker basket. She stopped next to Roger, holding the basket of clothes high on her hip, and looked up once quizzically at the light, shaking her head almost angrily.

"It's always red when ah gets heah, nev-ah green,"

she muttered. Then the light changed and she shot
off the curb, head down, still muttering, and Roger
saw his chance and went with her.

The cars were waiting for them to cross now and he
looked and saw the light they were facing wasn't red
but green. *I guess I should have figured that out.
That wasn't too tough to figure out, was it?* But before he could decide, he wondered should he ask that
mad old Negro woman if he could carry her basket
for her.

That's what I ought to do. He could see himself
asking and her handing him the basket, and he was
smiling, and then the next thing he was tripping,
and the clothes were flying all over the street, getting
dirtier by the minute. He wanted to apologize for
getting her clothes all dirty but she looked too angry.
Then suddenly he heard honking and cars bearing
down on him and he felt her strong hand grasp him
and as she yanked him along, she yelled, "C'mon,
chile, shake yo' leg!"

He wanted to thank her for probably saving his life
but she had dropped her arm the moment they
reached the curb and forgotten him completely, staring up at the street light of the side street.

"Same dam' thing," she muttered, "every time ah
aims to cross, dat dam' light's agin' me!"

Roger watched her light change to green. She put
her dark head down and charged across, walking
strongly with a wide waddling stride. He felt happy
and wanted to go after her and talk, but decided he'd
only get in the way and he'd better not. Then he

changed his mind, but by this time the street light
was red again so he gave up the idea and walked the
other way.

After the next corner he saw the light but turned
right instead and walked down the long street to another street light. He turned right again. At the next
corner there was another light and again he turned
right and walked along the street and now he saw he
was back where he had been. *Well, I guess it beats
worrying about the lights but where does it get me?*

He turned back to Second. When the people waiting for the light there crossed, he went along with
them. He kept doing that until he came to Madison
Avenue.

The streets had become more crowded as he walked
west. When, a little before noon, he reached Madison
and 57th Street it was as if the corner held all the
people and cars that could possibly be put there.

He heard the traffic before he saw it: a clanking,
clanging, hooting, whining assault that made him
want to hold his ears. Then he got used to it, and it
was a melody of sound, a churning pattern of noises
that held and framed the moving masses of people
and cars that extended in all directions as far as he
could see.

The sun was very bright for mid-December and
thousands of shining black windows winked down at
him. The skyscrapers loomed, reaching to the sky,
each one enormous and monolithic. Across the street,
a new building was going up, its skeleton decorated
with tiny men moving along girders in shining bell-
shaped hats; the harsh sounds of the pneumatic drills

punctuated the sounds of the traffic like exclamation points.

The air wasn't as good here as it had been near the river. The big green city buses released their fumes in clouds of yellow and gray, and he had to push his nose down in his wool scarf to breathe. The little cars slipped into their places, shifting gears, braking for the light, idling, moving side-by-side north and south, east and west, with yellow, red and green checkered taxis, trucks, blue mail and brown delivery vans.

Boy, what a mess, he thought, watching the thick, seemingly immovable line that stretched to the horizon move snakelike, stop and move and stop again, the pattern almost a ballet against the harsh symphony of sound.

He must have been in the way because people kept bumping and jostling him, in an unseeing matter-of-fact way. They came on like the tide, relentlessly forward, and he had to give ground and retreat finally to the entrance of a silver shop where there was a cold white granite pillar to hold on to. He tried to keep his elbows and feet in, to make himself as small as possible so that he wouldn't get swept away.

I could fall down, and they'd never know it. They'd walk all over me and flatten me out like a carpet. They don't see anything; they're just walking.

Into the shops and out they came, as if ejected by invisible jet streams, or into the high vaulted openings of the big office buildings as hundreds of others left.

At times they broke into little swirls with their

own rhythms, and went into the big hole with the sign over it that read SUBWAY; the ones coming out detached into little clusters at the corners, waiting for the lights to change; as they hurried across, others moved up to take their places.

It's like a parade going in all directions, without the band playing. All they need is the band and maybe they'd all move in the same direction. He felt like shouting to them to slow down here and hurry up there so they could all be together. But he didn't.

He noticed that the women carried packages held high on their bodies in their gloved hands, that the men carried their packages downward at the utmost extension of their arms, a lot of them with the exact same attache case in black or brown. It bothered him that there weren't any children.

I guess they're in school someplace. But it didn't occur to him that he wasn't, and he didn't bother himself thinking why.

The next time he looked up the street sign said Fifth Avenue on one side and 57th Street on the other. It wasn't quite as crowded. A burly policeman was standing in the center of the street wearing a long blue coat, waving his arms and blowing a whistle that he kept in his mouth, his cheeks very red and a lot of steam coming off his face. Roger thought he saw the policeman look at him one time when he waved his arms, but a turning car hit a small white metal sign that said NO LEFT TURN and the big policeman leaned down, very angry and blowing his steam right into the face of the driver of the wrong-turning car.

At 25th Street there was hardly any traffic and he

was looking inside the wire fence of a school at a lot
of girls playing ball in white shirts and black shorts.
Some of them were pretty good at throwing the ball.

He noticed that he was holding the wool scarf
ends against the cold steel fence to keep his hands
from sticking. That made him wonder about the girl
who gave it to him. She'd spoken of going to a school
where they played music; would they be allowed to
play ball at that kind of school? He looked around
quickly, but all these girls were running around and
jumping high in the air and he didn't think she was
able to do that so he walked away.

On the street where there were stables and high
stamping horses he wanted to stay and watch but
another policeman was standing inside talking, and
the horse shook his head, making it appear as if he
understood. *Now I'll probably have them both after
me,* Roger thought, and turned away before the
policeman could recognize him.

He was getting hungry. He didn't think he had any
money so he kept on walking. The next corner sign
said Avenue of the Americas. *What did the
Americas look like?* The street turned out to be one
of the shabbiest and dreariest of any he had walked
this day.

*I guess it's like that Nemo Newman pretending
she can walk.* He didn't jump up and down with joy
when her name slipped into his mind. All he said
was, *It's about time, dummy.*

He passed a lot of pawn shops and places to cash
your checks, then a little stand where a wonderful
tantalizing smell enveloped him. He saw the man

turning the frankfurters on his grill, and a homemade sign that said HOT DOGS but not how much. He reached into his pocket and a quarter was there. He held it out to the man.

"Can I get a hot dog for this?"

The man wearing a white jacket reached out and grabbed the quarter.

"For a quarter, Jack, you kin get one wit' mustard!" he said jovially and then he was smearing it on and adding a big wad of sauerkraut and Roger was so hungry when he took the hot dog that his hand was shaking.

He took one bite and then he heard a squealing of brakes and a hoarse voice yelling: "*Baxter!* Is that *you*, doll?"

CHAPTER EIGHTEEN

HEY, STUPID, wake up, somebody's calling you.

He turned and saw a yellow taxicab at the curb, a girl inside waving at him, her face, a pale oval, beautiful against the jet blackness of her hair. Her eyes were the unusual color of violet; her bright red lips seemed nonchalant or bored but there was a husky hoarse voice coming from between them.

"Baxter, is it *you*, love?"

The hot dog in his hand was forgotten, but the spume inside his head all this day was still congealed and reluctant to dissolve.

I'm pretty sure that's a familiar face.

Yeah, sure, but who? Remember, it spoke to us first so I guess we're not exactly strangers.

I think I know. It's somebody we like.

I know that, stupid, but who? Who?

I don't know who. Don't rush me. All I know is I know her.

Okay, so if you know her, it stands to reason you've got to know who it is, right?

His head hurt when he tried shaking it.

I think it's that Egyptian princess.

Oh, that's great! You're just the one who knows Egyptian princesses.

Honest, she's the one. Don't you remember?

I only remember what you remember, dummy.

He made himself take another step forward, then another until he was standing so near the cab he could reach out and touch her. Now he could even smell that he knew her.

It's a special kind of flower. Not azaleas or roses. It's sort of like lilacs. Or maybe it's like lemon or orange blossoms. . . .

Will you cut it out? he heard himself yelling inside. *Stop with the flower program. Who is it? Who? Who?*

Suddenly he saw her face very clearly and her eyes were smiling directly into his.

"Hi, Baxter," she said. "Long time, no see."

He shook his head almost angrily again and suddenly everything seemed to become crystal clear. The thick spume inside his head had vanished, triggered by his heart beating strongly inside him. Then he heard a voice he knew was his saying:

"Hey! Hi, Miss Bentley!"

"What are you doing way down here, doll? Come on, I'll give you a lift home."

The rear door of the cab opened and her black-gloved hands got hold of his scarf ends and she was reeling him in, landing him as if he were some kind of a fish. He stumbled in, holding on to his hot dog, careful not to spill any of it on her, feeling warm and foolish.

"Sam," she yelled suddenly, "do you smell what I do? It's a hot dog!"

He saw she was addressing the grizzled cab driver, who needed a shave and had white hairs showing on his face. It was the kind of stubble he remembered his mother yelling about.

"No," he heard his father saying, "I didn't shave. Is it in my contract here that I must shave every day?"

"Maybe not but you look like a bum," she answered.

Then he heard Miss Bentley's voice starting to say something. She had to stop and cough. He felt her hand tighten on his arm. When she stopped, her face was very close to his and she was looking at him almost beseechingly.

"Can I have a bite, Baxter? I'm starving." She was looking, all eyes, at the hot dog in his hand. "Come on, lover, give."

He grinned and held it out for her, her red mouth open ready to bite into it as she leaned forward. He noticed her lips looked wet. *Gosh, she's pretty. She's prettier than any movie star I ever saw, and I sure saw lots of them. . . .*

Some friends or clients of his father's were coming into the big Brentwood house with all the bathrooms. Looking down from the balcony just above the curving red-carpeted steps, he could see their hair, very carefully set and shining, and then their heads would tilt and they were hugging or kissing his father. Then he saw his mother, also with her hair up, hugging the stars too or kissing them on the cheek. Then some men came in and everybody was hugging and kissing everybody, all in a pretty good mood with the loud laughing that he liked. Sometimes a star looked up at him and made a funny face and said, "Who's that?" and then they heard something and said, "Oh," and the smile went away and then they took off their coats and went inside and he was still up there hiding behind the white stair-rails.

Her beautiful face drew back from his with a disappointed look. "I forgot I've got this utterly fantastic cold, doll, and I don't want to give it to you." She looked at the hot dog greedily. "Okay if we divvy it up?"

His head was a yo-yo again, nodding and bobbing. *Come on, talk!* he shrilled inside at himself, but he was too busy watching her face.

Boy, it's too bad she's only a model. What a terrific movie star she'd make. She'd be better than all of them. Her face changes expression a million times a minute. Maybe I could get her a job out there. My pop could sure use her. Even though she's too good to waste on that dumb Jerry Jeeks. . . .

They were coming into the office and his father was sitting at the big black desk pretending to be busy writing something on that ruled yellow pad.

"This is Miss Bentley, Pop," he heard himself say.

She was standing there tall and straight and proud and looking so beautiful he knew she had to get the contract. He noticed there was a slight smile on her lips, not too much, almost as if she was amused about something. Maybe it's his hair, he thought. I guess he can use one of those wigs, or rugs, like they say.

Then his father was looking up, appearing very tired and mad about something. "Yes?" he said, "What is it?"

He's not interested, he thought. *He's mad at me again for interrupting. But that's only because I'm not a certain well-known comic.*

"Pop, she's a good friend of mine, a very famous model, and I figured you could use her in some of your pictures."

He noticed she was coughing again. *Please don't do that,* he wanted to tell her. *They got a terrible thing about colds here. They're all afraid of germs. Don't cough, please.*

But she kept on coughing.

Hold it just a minute, he said silently to her, *I want to see what happens.*

His father, standing in front of her, his cigar clenched in his teeth, was still mad because he was saying, "Well, say something. Just don't

stand there. I'm busy. Hurry up, I've got a lot
on my mind."

I'm sorry, he wanted to tell her. *Look, I'm
awful sorry. That's the way he is. Only I thought
he'd make an exception in your case.*

He heard the phone ring and his father excuse
himself, "That's for me." Then his father's eyes
cut them off. "Yes, Jerry," he said. "What's new,
kid? What? Oh, nothing much. The kid just
dropped in with a friend and I was just telling
him—what? Oh, no, I can talk. What's up?"

And then he was making the familiar sign
with his hand that said so long, see you later,
close the door on your way out.

*I could have told you that would happen,
dope*, he scolded himself, looking at her to see if
she was disappointed too. But she was smiling.

Then he saw she was holding the hot dog in her
hand, not worrying if the mustard and sauerkraut got
on her gloves; she got it around the middle and
winked at him as she broke it in half. She handed
him his.

"Eat hearty," she said and lifted her half as if it
were a glass she was saying "Cheers" to before gulping it down. She rolled her eyes as she ate and he was
so happy watching her enjoyment that he forgot he
was still holding his own half uneaten.

She had hardly finished when she started coughing
again. Then she took a deep breath and sighed and
patted his hand with her glove.

"Baxter, that was delicious. Absolutely the most

wonderful meal I ever ate. And if you want to know
what's wrong with this country, I'll tell you—they've
forgotten what it means to dine graciously. M-mmm!"
she finished purring.

The driver was still sitting there patiently waiting.

"Sam," she said, "it was great! Do you want one?"

"Sure I want one," he said, "but my stomach don't.
Those dogs kill me."

"Okay," she said. "Then let's move it."

The cab shot away from the curb.

Sam Goldberg, the cabbie's hack license said. He
wondered how come she knew him well enough to
call him by his first name. There was a sign on the
seat separation that told him to lean back and enjoy
the ride. The cab picked up speed, weaved in and
around some big trucks expertly and he knew Sam
Goldberg was a good driver.

A little triangular stone park near 34th Street, with
a few benches and a lot of pigeons strutting around,
looked more like a park for grounded pigeons than
for people. The street was very congested, policemen were blowing whistles, and people running across
were dodging speeding cars to get to the big department stores here.

He saw Miss Bentley dabbing at her lips with a
flimsy scented handkerchief, then she was pointing
her black-gloved finger at his uneaten half of the hot
dog. She flicked imaginary crumbs from his face when
he was finished and seemed to be laughing inside.
Her face was usually inscrutable and you could tell
she was laughing only by watching her violet eyes.

"How's old Qu'est-ce que ca c'est?" he asked suddenly and her laughing response was immediate.

"Who—Roger?"

Then she had to cough again, a hacking dry cough that made her bend over. She wore a hip-high light tan cloth coat, open, and a black belted dress with a single strand of pearls at her throat. Her short narrow boots were fur-trimmed but when her slim silky legs touched his he could feel how cold they were.

When she finished coughing, she told him Roger was fine. "*I'm* dying right now but *he's* fine. As a matter of fact, he asked about you the other day."

Who, me? He thought of the big man, Roger Tunnell, with his stiffly held neck and wished he could see him again. He wondered if they were going to get married.

I bet if I had a father like him, none of these dumb things would happen to me.

He remembered one of the first letters he had written God: "Hey, how come you let them do these things? It's about time you paid attention to what's going on." He signed it Your friend, Roger Baxter.

And another one: "Thanks a lot for what you let Her do to me yesterday. He didn't seem to care much. You know. I don't want you to strike them down dead exactly but how about some lightning and thunder to scare them a little? My friend Adam tells me you're probably on a vacation. Maybe you ought to hurry back." He signed this one R.B.

The honking of horns and screeching of brakes made him look up to see Sam trying to make a left hand turn.

"No, Sam," he heard her say. "Through the park. Let's make it a big deal."

The cabbie swung obediently back into line. Ahead was a low wall. He headed for the opening in it, went through and turned right into the drive. A lot of large rocks jutted out from the grassy slopes above them, and then began a continual curve with light signals at intervals.

She was asking him if he had ever been in Central Park and he had to shake his head No. So she leaned toward his side of the window and pointed out the ice skaters going around, some of them girls wearing short flaring skirts, some others, older, were skating more upright, the men wearing scarves under their coats and the women colorful hats.

"Ice skating in the winter, boating in the summer on the lake," she told him. "A great zoo, too. In fact, if I didn't have this crazy cold today I'd take you there right now to see the polar bears and seals. They've a bird house and a snake-and-monkey house and lions, tigers, camels, elephants—everything. Did I leave anything out, Sam?"

"Yeah," the cabbie grunted. "Tell him to bring a gun when he comes."

The park drive curved toward Fifth Avenue and then swung away. A big stone cat perched on a big rock looked almost live enough to spring, scaring him some until he saw it was a statue. Another one, of a husky, had a plaque under it telling how this dog brought the serum that time and saved those Alaskans.

Well, I'm glad they care about dogs here. He suddenly remembered Olvera Street in the Mexican quarter of Los Angeles where they held that ceremony sixteen centuries old that allowed children and adults to bring their animals for blessing once a year. . . .

"Almighty Father, we bless these animals for all they have done for us, with clothing and companionship, and rendering a service to the human race since time began," the Padre said loudly, standing on the narrow cobblestoned street. And then they brought along the black satin cow with the crown of orchids and the blanket of gardenias. The *Benediction de los Animales,* it said on the sign. His friend Joey was going with his dog and said his father would take him along too if he wanted.

"How come I don't got a dog?" he asked both parents.

"That's all we need here," She said. "You're not enough."

All of the other animals and people followed in line after the black satin cow that Joey's father said was a Holstein, the people all dressed up even if a lot of them were very poor. He never knew Joey's parents were Mexican and called him José, a name he didn't use in school.

"*Por favor,*" he heard Joey say to the Padre when he lifted up the small head-turning cocker spaniel who was more interested in the other animals. It was a cold day in March and he himself was shivering because he didn't want to wear a coat that was too new and shiny.

"That's Cleopatra's Needle," he heard Pat Bentley say, and he looked up in time to see a high white stone pointed at the top like the Washington Monument. He had seen pictures of that. Obelisk, it was called.

She pointed out the Museum of Art nearby, then the ball fields, and when the drive headed west he was so fascinated by the mid-city skyline he forgot he was heading for home. Her next sentence reminded him.

"I guess you've got a big date to be cutting school so early," she said teasingly.

They were swinging on to Central Park West, and then the cabbie turned and it was 86th Street. He wanted to explain but didn't know how.

She'll only think you're some kind of a nut. Besides, how can I tell her when I don't even know myself?

Out loud he said finally, "I guess I just felt like going."

She didn't disappoint him. "I couldn't begin to count my hooky days in school." She included the driver in her conversation again. "How about you, Sam? Did you cut school much?"

The cabbie made a short derisive laugh. "Who knew from school in dose days—I bin woikn' sinct I was thoiteen."

Roger thought he detected a kinship between the way Sam talked and the first cabbie he'd heard that time with the model and Roger Tunnell.

"Is he—Sam—fwom Bwooklyn, too?"

The cabbie turned his head to stare at Roger, ignoring traffic. "What Brooklyn?" he grunted with contempt. "Dat's pure Noo Yawk yer hearin', buddy. Hell's Kitchen I'm from. Right in da heart. Them Brooklyns," he said wagging his head as if bewildered, "dey tawk a sepprit lan'witch dere."

I can't tell them apart. I guess I'll have to talk to more people here to tell the difference.

Yeah, he answered himself mockingly, *You do that.*

They crossed Broadway, went downhill past Park and there still weren't any kids his age around. Then she was in another coughing fit that lasted the long block home.

Sam swung the cab in toward the curb as they neared the corner. "You better watch it," he said. "Dere's a lotta dis flu aroun'!"

"Not any more," she gasped. "I've got it all."

She was opening her thin black bag and taking money out. She gave the driver a bill and he looked at it and handed it back, telling her she needed glasses.

"You forgot," she said. "I made five hundred smackeroos today. Let's share the wealth."

"Crazy, ya gotta be crazy," Sam said, shaking his head. He was wearing an old beat-up cap and no tie and a light windbreaker over his sweater.

Her gloved hand touched Roger's scarf. "I like your scarf," she said, patting it smooth. "Aren't you ever getting an overcoat? This isn't L.A., you know."

He told her he probably would some day. She still wasn't in any hurry to get out of the taxi.

"What's your mother going to say when you come

home so early? You're not sick or anything, are you?"

He shook his head. She had a point there though.

"Maybe you ought to go someplace, doll. You know, kill a little time. A movie, maybe. Or a museum?"

What was the name of the place that Nemo Newman had mentioned? Then he remembered and asked was there a Modern Museum someplace?

The violet eyes of the model were turning red-rimmed finally with all that coughing. "Modern Museum?" she replied. "Great. That's on 53rd, doll. Sam will take you. Okay, Sam?"

The grizzled man said, "Whatever you say, beautiful."

Roger was remembering he had spent his last quarter on the hot dog, and she must have read his mind for she was pressing the folded green bill inside his outer chest pocket. He drew back, not wanting to take it. Her hands went to her narrow hips then in simulated outrage.

"Didn't you split your hot dog with me?" and he had to nod his head. "Well, then, okay," she said, "so now we're even." Then she was walking away and he hadn't even said thanks and the grinning red-faced doorman was out there to usher her inside the revolving glass doors.

Then she did a strange wonderful thing that he was not to forget. She stopped in the middle of the walk suddenly and struck a pose. Her gloved hand found her flowing hip, the other hand thrown up and outward, and she did something with her feet that put her into a graceful swayed position, freezing there instantly—and he knew it was for him, as if he were a photographer. It was long enough for him to say CLICK in his mind and when the shutter flew she knew it and blew him a kiss, all very deadpan and nonchalant.

Then Sam was turning the big cab out, spinning his wheels in a wide sweeping U-turn on the wide street, picking up speed as his automatic gears changed.

Hold it, please hold it another second, until she is gone.

But when he looked back, almost frantically turning his head, all he could see were the spinning glass doors of the apartment building glinting in the sun's light.

CHAPTER NINETEEN

NOBODY WAS THERE to spin the doors for him at the Modern Museum and he went in at his own pace, pushing steadily with his hands on the glass and then when he was in letting go and the doors spun without him.

Okay, here we are. Now *what?*

Afterward he would wait in the cold north wing lobby of his building, hoping the girl Nemo would come along and see him still wearing her scarf. He would wait a long time but she never would come in time to hear about his visit to the Museum.

He wanted to tell her it was a good place to go apart from the pictures and paintings and abstract sculpture. It was the wild style of the kids who congregated there later, in their suede and leather boots, their leg-long laced moccasins and loafers, the girls mini-skirted with purple and pink and white legs or with knee-socks of blue and green and their hair

worn crazy, the boys with flopping shirts over tapered
slacks and levis, golf sweaters under parkas or pea
coats or corduroys, hair long like the Beatles or the
Animals or the Things, mod-belted. Only a few were
square and old-time-collegiate groomed, straight and
silly without the imagination or humor of the others
who could have been putting everybody on, the crazy
sunglasses and pale lipsticks and stick-on lashes out
to there.

He liked and envied the way they took over and
made this Museum their own. They all had the
magic mouth and although they were a slightly
older group he couldn't imagine them ever without
it. He didn't notice any outcasts like himself slink-
ing around. The large groups evidently came from
different schools and swirled in their own eddies as
they jammed the halls and stairways, the girls from
the parochial schools with their uniform dress—the
plaid skirts and dark blue coats and white blouses—
more restrained, not as psychedelic or turned-on as
the others.

He checked for elevators so she would have no
trouble. There were two, for three walking flights up
and two below the main lobby where they checked
the museum member cards and sold tickets for their
art movies; and when you paid, the smiling Negro
in the neat uniform let down the padded silken rope
chained to the metal post.

He found Picasso and Gris and Bonnard and the
eye-slanted women of Modigliani and the primitive
Rousseau with his smooth night on the endless desert,

the lion and the sleeping man wearing the colored striped robe not caring about the lion and the lion the same. He passed the op and pop rooms and saw an Arp with a hole in its white purity that he liked and the landscapes of Cezanne.

A burst of laughter from a group of kids crowded near a painting brought him circling back. They were looking at the Great Nude of Modigliani, the typical eye-slant not so noticeable in the profile of the woman stretched on the divan. They all had some comment.

A boy about fifteen said innocently enough, "That's what you like, isn't it, Harry?"

"*Mama mia!*" The boy Roger guessed was Harry made an exaggerated whistling sound.

"Hey, Norma," another said, "how'd they get your picture?"

"That's not me, you dope. Are you blind? That's my mother."

Then a serious-faced girl wearing brilliant blue leotards and a short skirt said, "It's not *that* funny, you creeps. Modigliani suffered all his life."

"Yeah, I'll bet. I'd sure like to suffer with that kind of stuff around."

"I can always tell one of his paintings from his eyes."

"Who's looking at her eyes?"

The breasts of the reclining nude were great circles of lightly tinted flesh tones changing to yellows. She looked completely relaxed on the reddish divan and Roger wondered if she was a girl friend of Modigliani.

He heard one in the laughing group say the artist died very young and there was a jesting answer to that as he moved away.

There were some other nudes he didn't like as much, the bulky brick-red Renoirs, and the long twisted Matisse ones.

There were two Van Goghs he did like: The countryside at night, with the little houses and the moon outlined in heavy blue, the curling vivid parallel strokes of blue and green churning the sky making it seem to move and the stars twinkling red and remote. The other was the red-rimmed eye of the artist, a self-portrait, holding him with its strange cold lost face and the funny hat he didn't know he was wearing.

In another room one entire wall was covered with a cluster of wood all colored the same tone of gray, the wood piled high as if carelessly set or thrown there, some with nails still in them and others merely broken or nailed together without matching. It was a jumble that seemed to make sense and although he never knew that anything like that would be in a museum or even be called art, he liked the idea. *Nobody's cracking the whip over* her, that's for *sure,* he said to himself as he read her name on the small white card: Louise Nevelson. He had an idea he'd like to make something like that.

A great white painting with fierce thrusting diagonals painted in thick slashes frightened him. The artist's name was Franz Kline. *What's he mad about?*

He saw the sad guitars of Bracque and the white doves and black shadows of simple birds, the ballet girls of Degas, the colorful crowded studio of Matisse, the geometrics of Mondrian, and he wondered, *Where have I been all this time?* Then he stood in front of the Miró fantasies and the swirling paint streaming over the Jackson Pollock and the washers and cigarette butts in there too, and when he came to the big gray Guernica of Picasso suddenly it was all too much for him and he thought he'd better get out of there before somebody asked him what was the matter.

Some college kids were leaving when he stopped to pick up his books at the ground level checkroom. A torn scrap of yellow paper fluttered to the floor and he bent to pick it up. He was about to call to the group just going out the revolving doors, but the woman checker was repeating, "Are these yours? Are these yours?" as she held out his books. He didn't know if he was supposed to give her a tip or what, so he looked quickly to see what the others were doing and by that time the college group had gone.

He unfolded the scrap of paper. It had the thin ruled green lines on yellow of a composition book, almost like the kind He always used for his notes only that came off a legal pad.

He read it again and had the feeling it had come off some students' bulletin board where they must leave notes to each other.

He wasn't sure what it was all about but he liked the friendly feeling about it. He folded it again and placed it on top of the checkroom table when the woman attendant's back was turned and everybody else too happy and busy talking to notice. *Maybe*

Bull Cow —

Shudder, quake —
I have a Geog lab
final, so I don't
have much time
to groove this morning
Darlene —

DAN —
neither do I got
a math midterm (MIDTERM?)
this aft and have to
figure out what's
happening — finally
over which way math to go →
Narin HOLY
COW!

HOLY COW D+K!
I'VE GOT
FAITH IN
BOTH OF YOU —
YOU CAN DO IT!
Affectionately (wow)
BULL COW DAN

thanx DAN
but that didn't
help me much
in math
K.

Karin will come back for it. Or maybe the other one, Darlene. It could be that Bull cow Dan.

Okay, maybe you're right for once. I agree. It could be. Now can you guess what She's going to do? No!

Later, he remembered them all hip and groovy and cool, at ease in their teen roles. He could still hear their chatter punctuated by explosive laughter uninhibited and loud even in the Museum and nobody shooshing them as they squealed, fighting some of the cornier paintings like he did the TV commercials.

Bull. That was what those commercials were. Just bull.

Even the grown-up commercials were. Just bull.

Even the grown-up commercials were phoney. All those dopey women at the washing machines pretending their wash was whiter than the others. The men suddenly without a cigarette and the other fellow saying, Here, try one of mine, and when he did, with the smoke coming out of his nose and mouth, saying, "M-mmmmm but this is *good!*" or tastier or fresher or more fragrant. You could see he was never going to touch his old rotten brand again.

Yeah, yeah. Sure you dope. This one is gold.

They all had the new miracle ingredient added. KS 2 or BS 4 or XK 9 or the big long scientific hybridwords that made things last longer or shine brighter or settle your aching stomach faster or your nagging headache in half the time, and if you used any of these you had a beautiful house with no dust dirt or grime and the kids all were shining and clean and no animal dared to roll in the mud and you could see how happy and loving they all were, not to mention successful with their cars and the men hugging their wives when they came home, not the least bit sore or tired or busy now, but just happy.

Yeah, sure. Tell me some more lies. Pretending.

Like what She was telling him now. It was pretty clear She hadn't forgotten the ripped out telephone, no sir. She hadn't forgotten anything. About how he was a rope around Her neck and a weight nobody could bear and She didn't need him and could be happy without him and the only reason She took him after the separation was the father didn't want him either and the only other choice was to send him to a home.

You wouldn't want that, would you?

Always, always. She's pretending too, like the commercials, like the way everybody lies, right?

Well, now, I'm not so sure.

Look at Her eyes. I know you hate to do it but go on look and tell me what you see. Not love, right?

So what if She's not pretending?

Like it's happening to you, baby.

She must have been waiting near the door listening for the elevator and his footsteps because She hit him the moment he stepped inside the apartment. As his books went flying all he could think of was what a dope he was to forget She would be there. She never forgot.

He asked Her if She felt better now and She hit him again and he fell back, his head slamming the door.

CRUNCH, *that ought to do it.*

Maybe that's why that Modigliani died young. Maybe his mother killed him. I'll have to read up on him. Maybe he had a good reason.

Another name flashed into his mind. Arshile Gorky. He could still see the little white card at the museum saying the artist killed himself, not too long ago. *I wonder why. He must have had some pretty big problems. I thought painting made you happy.*

"—so you had to call your father and complain," She was saying in that lumpy Texas voice.

I don't know how you ever won Miss Texas. I wouldn't even vote you Miss Living Room.

Then he heard some more about teaching him a lesson so when She went inside to get something he decided he didn't want any more lessons and went out the door. He didn't bother taking the elevator down. It was only eighteen floors.

CHAPTER TWENTY

HE MUST have walked up past Park and Broadway for he was now at the corner of Central Park West, with the park ahead of him. He crossed with the light and pedestrians ducking the in-turning crosstown traffic.

There were large gray rocks looming high over the park entrance there but no crouching stone animals. He went in and climbed the rocks and dropped off at the other side, which should have been more fun than it was.

He walked a little way along a curving esplanade and heard a steady rhythmic slapping sound. He looked up away from his feet and saw some kids inside a concrete court playing handball.

He ducked under an overpass to a narrow turf-like trail lined with bushes, some still with patches of the dry glittering snow that clung to the sides sloping away. He had forgotten the snow. Now he saw it dully; it had no meaning for him.

He was walking south but didn't care much, just slogging across the path watching the soft clods of turf his feet kicked up. He became slowly aware of a soft thudding sound coming up fast behind him with an odd filliping rhythm, *Broomp Broomp Broomp*, and he wondered what it was. Suddenly it was almost upon him with another rasping sound of heavy breathing and a strange animal cry. He turned to look over his shoulder and fell back out of the way, twisting his body.

The girl on the horse was leaning forward, her gloved hands thrust at the horse's neck, her cloth-covered seat rising and falling in unison with the animal's gallop.

A girl riding a horse, that's all it is.

Okay, so now you know.

She probably would have smiled but it was too cold. She went by looking grim, holding the reins. He watched her coattails flying and her posting, up and down, the galloping hooves throwing up thick clods of turf, until the trail curved out of view. The thudding thinned until at last there was only the sound of his own breathing.

A stone-covered walk curved and took him out of the park. He found another one, and that curved and out again, too. Then he forgot about the park and walked toward the high buildings silhouetted dark and purple against the setting sun. When he reached 59th Street it was dark and the purple was gone.

Strange red-clad figures with straggly white beards rang bells on corners but not until he reached Fifth Avenue did he realize he was seeing a different Santa Claus at each corner and that it was Christmas music being piped out of the stores he passed. He heard Silent Night, and voices singing *Oh Come Ye to Bethlehem*. He saw the big cards that said PEACE ON EARTH GOOD WILL TOWARD MEN and the red-clad rednosed men shook their bells and people dropped money into their black pots. Everybody was singing softly and sweetly and the PEACE ON EARTH cards multiplied.

Yeah, yeah. Once a year they remember. It sure doesn't last long. Peace on earth my foot.

Nobody told me it was getting to be Christmas. No wonder there's so many people shopping and carrying presents.

He saw a woman ahead of him carrying a lot of packages and pulling a little boy, who stumbled and fell. She swore and yanked him to his feet. Then she transferred her packages so she could have her right arm free to hit the kid. He cried and she yelled crossly at him. He fell again, she yanked him up, switched her packages and smacked the boy once more hard. He was about four. And nobody noticed.

There's a lot of peace on earth going on!

Near the corner the whole sequence happened a third time. But when she tried shifting packages she dropped a few and in trying to catch those dropped the rest of them.

Roger stooped for the packages. Thank you, thank

you, she was saying as he handed them to her. The little boy was still crying when he picked up the last and largest box, so heavy he wondered how she could carry that and the others so easily. *I guess she's awful strong.* It felt like it had bricks in it.

As he gave it to her, he said, "Why don't you hit him with this? That ought to keep him quiet next time he falls."

Her slack mouth gaped fish-open and he could smell her harsh hot breath.

"Why you damn stinking little snot," she raged, "What do you know about bein' a mother?"

Then she bent down to the kid and belted him such an extra hard one that he fell down. She yanked him up, turning her head to glare viciously at Roger.

"He can thank *you* for that one, wise guy," she said and strode off pulling the bellowing boy, the crowded avenue of night shoppers parting like a wave to let her by.

I guess I should have kept my dumb mouth shut at that. Maybe now she'll send him to bed without supper. Maybe she's got her own lessons.

The brightly lit and decorated store window drew him closer. Its name looked familiar when he took a step back to gaze up at its ten-foot-high lights: APPLETON'S.

"This must be Dudley's old man's," he said aloud.

He stepped forward again to look at the Christmas gifts in the window. He ought to be getting some stuff too for people, he thought, feeling the five dollar bill his friend the model had given him still in his pocket. He walked inside the store with a quick happy feeling warming him through.

A small sign said OPEN UNTIL NINE and he shrugged. *I got nowhere to go.*

In his mind's eye, he saw them all clearly, the ones he would buy the gifts for: Nemo Newman, Marion Johnson, Roger Tunnell, Pat Bentley, Roberta Clemm.

Are you sure that's all? Better make sure. Maybe you forgot somebody.

Like who?

How do I know who? It's your money.

Who else do I know? Maybe you'd like me to get something for Mr. Sarcastic?

You mean Rawling?

I don't care. Like I said, it's your money.

You know who I really would like to get something for?

No, I give up.

That poor dumb Karin.

Who?

You know, the one that flunked her math that I found on that yellow piece of scrap paper.

Yeah, that would be nice. Do you know where she lives?

No, as a matter of fact, I don't. I don't even know her last name.

Okay, then. I'll give you good free advice. Don't send her any.

He walked around the ground level aisles of the

big glaring white department store trying to get close enough to see what was on the counters. The grown-up Christmas shoppers jammed the space and made believe they didn't see him trying to get through.

It's okay. It's like the commercials you like. You're all pretending.

He had to shake his head at some of the prices.

No wonder that kid Dudley's got the Rolls, the prices his old man asks. Boy, he really skins 'em, but good. Maybe they got better prices in the back.

When he got there they didn't. He looked around, the lights hurting his eyes, the din hurting his ears, the moving, bustling, jostling, grown-up, colorful crowd jangling his nerves somehow. He saw people waiting for elevators and then he saw the escalators, the people on them seemingly suspended in mid-air. He would escalate, too, he decided.

Upstairs little kids waited in line to meet a big jolly Ho-Ho-ing Santa Claus type, and he couldn't remember if he ever did that.

He wandered around looking at the toys and spent some time watching the electric trains. A salesman with a pale tired face came over. "See anything you want, kid?"

Roger shook his head.

"Okay. Then how's about movin' it—yer wastin' valuable space."

Peace on earth. He's only pretending too. That he's a human being.

"How much is that one?" he asked suddenly, loudly.

"Fifty bucks," the salesman said, half-interested.

He pointed to the larger set. "How much for that one?"

The salesman caressed its shining black sides. He looked down at Roger with a respectful air. "One hundred dollars. You want it?"

"Is that the best one you got?"

"Yes, sir. Would you like it?"

"I dunno," he said sleepily.

The salesman narrowed his eyes. "Say, are you sure you've got the money for this?"

"Money? I got money. Look." He took out the bill and the salesman looked at it and became very tired again.

"Five bucks? Get lost, willya?"

Roger watched him walk away and shrugged. He moved to another section. A woman standing at a corner wearing a heavy dark mink coat happened to see him. Then she looked in the opposite direction. Her hand stole out and grabbed a football from the counter and quickly shoved it inside her coat, and she patted it. Then her eyes were momentarily startled by seeing him still there. Her face froze, her expression became mean, and he thought she was going to yell at him. But she just gave him a look as if he were dirt, tossed her head and walked away.

Well, anyway, she means well. She's gettin' her kid a football.

He saw a few other shoplifters after that taking smaller things, slipping them inside their wide sleeves or their gloves. *That one with the football was the best, though it's a good thing the kid doesn't like skis.*

He kept walking through the store, going around and farther up, without finding anything he had enough money for that would take care of all of them. He was getting very tired and then he was in the furniture department and he sat down on one of the big easy chairs.

I'll just rest my bones here for awhile, and then we'll figure out what to do next.

He flicked his eyes open a few hours later to find the store dark, but he had forgotten where he was and kept on sleeping.

CHAPTER TWENTY-ONE

Two POLICEMEN cruising Central Park found him the next day sitting hunched up on the cold ground near the lake. They asked him what he was doing there and he said he didn't know. Then he said he wasn't sure but he was trying to save this duck from drowning.

"What duck?" they asked frowning.

He told them there *was* one all right. He didn't know his name when they asked him, or where he lived or how old he was. Maybe three or four, he said, but he wasn't sure. They told him he'd better come with them and he asked what if the duck came back and drowned. They told him ducks could swim, they didn't drown. He thought about it. Then he shook his head and asked what if they were only pretending.

"This one's either out of his head or he's got amnesia," one of them said. The other thought maybe both. In their car he asked who they were and they told him policemen. He didn't believe them and when they asked why, he said, "Lalala."

They couldn't find anything in his clothing that identified him and they drove him to a place with the name Bellevue Hospital. The larger of the two cops took him inside and told him not to worry.

"Worry," he said, "what's that?"

The policeman asked him again who his mother and father were and he kept flapping the ends of his long scarf instead of answering. A man in a long white coat came out and talked to him.

The big policeman asked before he left, "What did you call that again, doc?"

"Imperception."

Then he was inside a room and a nurse wearing white shoes helped him undress. Then they were shining a light in his eyes and the man doing it had very thick lenses without rims. He asked him which was his right hand and he said he didn't know, he'd have to guess.

"Where is your belly?" the doctor asked and he pointed to his left hand.

"Where is your heart?" He pointed to his left hand.

The doctor touched Roger's knee. "What's this?"

"Elbow."

He touched his nose. "And this?"

"Ear."

The doctor put his hand on his own forehead. "What's this?" Roger thought for a while and then said he thought it was a chin.

The doctor handed him a pencil and a piece of paper. "Write your name," he said.

Roger's hand dropped the pencil.

"What is your name?"

"I don't know."

"Can you count?"

"I don't know."

"Will you try?"

He counted on his fingers, 1,2,3,4,5 and then on his other hand 6,7,8,9,10.

"What comes after ten?"

"I don't know."

"How much are two and two?"

"I don't know."

"One and one?"

"I don't know."

The doctor showed him a watch. "What's this?" He said, "I don't know."

Then he showed him a pen. "What's this?"

Roger said, "I don't know." Then he said, "No, it's a key."

He showed him a key and Roger said it was a pen. He didn't know what a chair was. Then he said it might be a table. The doctor showed him his eyeglasses and asked what they were but Roger didn't know.

"How do you feel?" he asked.

"Feel? What does that mean?"

The doctor asked him to draw a triangle and he drew a square. For a square he drew a triangle. For a diamond he drew a circle.

"Which is the right side of your body?"

"I don't know."

"Put your right hand on your hips."

Roger raised his right hand and then stopped it in mid-air. "I don't know," he said.

"Can you recite the alphabet?"

"I don't know what you mean."

The doctor recited the alphabet for him. "Is that familiar to you?"

At first he made no response. Then he said, "Z—I don't know."

"Did you ever hear it before?"

"No."

The doctor then asked him if he could write numbers and at first he said he didn't know, then he said he wasn't sure. The doctor put the pencil in his hand and asked him to write the number two. He wrote, 11.

"Four?"

He counted on his fingers and wrote, 1111.

"Nine?"

He wrote, 111111111.

The doctor pushed the pencil and paper away. "Are you worried about anything?"

"What does that mean—worried? I can't think —nothing."

"How do you feel?"

"Feel?"

"Would you like to talk to anybody you know?"

"Talk?"

"Do you think you're sick?"

"Sick?"

"Would you like to go home?"

"Home? Wait till I think." He sat there, eyes vacant.

"Well? Have you made up your mind?"

"Ur," Roger said.

"Ur? What does that mean?" the doctor asked him.

"I don't know."

The doctor examined Roger's eyes again, his ears, his chest, tongue and mouth. He stood him, he sat him, had him walk about and move all parts of his body. He explained about reflexes as he tested, said all were normal, as were Roger's responses to touch, pain, vibration and position. The doctor then took his temperature and examined his skull bones.

When he was all finished he smiled at Roger. Then he leaned over his report sheet, and Roger saw him write: *Amnestic syndrome. Imperception. Psychogenic body image disturbance with Aphasia and Agnosia.*

The doctor frowned at the space where it indicated NAME OF PATIENT.

"I guess we'll have to call you John Doe."

Roger knew what a doe was. He thought of his fawn. He remembered its lovely delicate head dipping to lap the water.

"Go ahead," he whispered. "Drink the water. You look awfully hot and tired."

He didn't see the doctor put his pen down. His eyes were far away on the fawn. . . .

He saw the slim legs spread, forelegs canted in the strange awkward angle. Then, while he was

wondering what to feed him, wondering if it
could be greens or berries, wondering if the fawn
would take them, wondering if he could spare
the time—the fawn's slender head came up and
his soft liquid eyes stared into Roger's. The damp
velvety nostrils quivered and his neck stretched
with his turning head to follow the fire high in the
hills. He struck the stone of the terrace with his
hooves and then he was walking silently across
the lawn.

"No," Roger whispered, "don't go yet. It's still
awfully hot back there. And there's an awful lot
of smoke."

He saw the deer dip his head twice as if in
grateful salute and then the quivering legs walking unsteadily toward the high hedge near the
bleeding heart tree. His head was held high now,
his nostrils sniffing and searching. Then his
haunches gathered, trembling, and he was soaring over the high hedge in a long graceful leap
toward the dark pall of smoke that densely
blanketed the forest beyond.

"No," he said. He was on his feet now watching the disappearing fawn, straining against the
curling wreaths of smoke. "Don't go back there.
It's still not safe. Everything's blistering hot. You'll
burn your feet, fawn."

And then he knew the fawn was going back to
his family, that he had to go even if he was going to die there. His teeth chattered and he was
suddenly very cold. He sat down clutching his
arms close to his chest and rocking. . . .

He felt something touch him and saw a long white coat.

"What did you say your name was?" he heard somebody ask.

"I don't got a name," he said. Then, "Ask Roberta Clemm. She knows all about it."

When the doctor asked him who Roberta Clemm was he growled like a tiger.

"Gr-r-rr!" he said. "That's who."

He looked up at the heavyset woman with the hair floppy and high on her head and the pugnacious smile.

"How we doing?" she asked him.

"I guess they put me in jail finally," he said.

She made her head turn slowly and deliberately as she looked around the small room. She walked over to the door she had closed quietly behind her and tapped it. It made a solid sound. Then she walked over to the far wall and tapped that too.

"I don't think so," she said. "I don't see any bars here. Whatever gave you that idea?"

He looked down at the white flannel nightshirt he was wearing and shrugged. Then he asked her, "What did you do?"

"I didn't do anything. What did you do?"

He shook his head very slowly. "I don't know."

Her good-natured bulk was reassuring to him. She sat down, massive and serene, as immovable as a mountain.

"I like you," he said. "You look solid."

"Thank you," she said. "That's nice. You look pretty good too."

He was squeezing his arms and his legs, in turn. Then he put his hands on his chest and rubbed it. "I don't know," he said. "I feel funny."

"What do you mean—funny?"

"Like there's nothing there—like I'm empty. Like I was always afraid of being. Out of it."

"Out of it?"

"Yeah. You know. No more." He turned his hands over, palms up, and looked at them dully. "But I don't think I am yet," he added. "Something's holding me."

"Well, whatever it is, hang on, sweetheart," she told him. "We don't want to lose people we like."

"Do I know the alphabet?" he asked her suddenly recognizing who she was through the affectionate tone of voice. "I think somebody asked me if I know the alphabet."

"Perhaps you do," Miss Clemm said. "But it isn't very important. Would you like to go to sleep now and rest?"

He told her the trouble was there were too many pictures going on and off in his head lately and they wouldn't settle down and be still.

"Noisy ones, too," he said. "I got 'em with sound. Like my own TV inside."

"With or without commercials?" she asked.

He didn't answer. He was already asleep. He slept for five minutes, then opened his eyes and stared at the ceiling. He moved his toes under the blanket and

looked at them for awhile. Then he raised his knees
and sat up and touched them.

"We're still here," he said without seeming to notice her and dropped off to sleep again. He slept for
ten more minutes, then got up and out of bed. He
nodded politely to her but didn't say anything. He
walked straight to the far wall and put his hands on
it and pushed hard.

"I've got to get out of here," he said. He looked
straight up at the ceiling as if measuring the height.
Then he went over to a chair and brought that back
with him. He was going to stand on it but then he
could see that it wasn't going to work and he walked
back and forth fretting about it. Then he sat down in
the chair and was lost in thought. He looked at Roberta Clemm sitting quietly across from him.

"We'll never make it," he told her. "We're locked
up tight. What we need is a window."

"Oh?" she asked. "Are we going out the window?"

He nodded soberly. "We gotta or they'll fink we
'tole the football! But she took it—in her coat. This
way." He pantomimed the shoplifter.

"Is this like the place where you spent the other
night?" she asked him and he thought about that for
a while.

"Boy, was I lost," he said.

He went back to the bed. "I guess we still got
some time be-fuh they open up. I think it's okay to
sleep."

She got up from her chair and put the blanket over
him nicely. "There's plenty of time," she told him.

"You get some rest now. I've got some things to do. I'll see you later."

His eyes flicked and looked searchingly into hers. "I think last time you took too long."

"I'm sorry," she said. "I didn't mean to. I'll do better this time. And please wait for me. I don't want to miss you."

"Okay," he said. "Okay. Okay, Miss Clemm. Miss Clemm—a-hum, a-hem."

"That's my name all right. You got that fine."

"You better wait for Miss Clemm this time," he told himself. He closed his eyes and was asleep very quickly.

Miss Clemm closed the door quietly. Then she walked down the corridor to an office where she looked at a slip of paper in her hand and picked up the telephone. She dialed the number and heard the ringing, and finally a woman's voice answered.

"Mrs. Baxter? This is Roberta Clemm speaking. Dr. Clemm. Your son's therapist at school."

"Oh? Well—he isn't here." The words were spoken with a southwestern inflection. Regional. Oklahoma or Texas, Miss Clemm thought.

"I know, Mrs. Baxter. He's here with me—at the hospital."

"Oh?"

She didn't ask what hospital. Or where. Or why.

"Aren't you interested in how Roger is?"

"What's that?"

"Do you know where your boy has slept the past two nights?"

"Look honey," Mrs. Baxter said, "if I tried to keep track of everything that kid did, I'd have gray hairs."

Miss Clemm frowned and tapped her pencil on the desk. "Yes. Children are a problem, aren't they?"

"I don't know about children. I just know he is."

"Well, then"—her fury was mounting but she made her voice even and cool—"I don't suppose you'd mind if we kept Roger here with us for a few more days—"

"Can you make it a week?"

Was she hearing correctly? she wondered.

The soft drawling voice continued. "You see I have a chance to go to Nassau with some friends—and as long as you're taking care of the kid anyway—"

"Look here," Miss Clemm said, her voice rising, "aren't you concerned about your son's condition?"

"Well, of course I am. But it'll keep, won't it?"

Miss Clemm jabbed the desk so hard the pencil point broke. She flicked the lead out with her finger.

"I mean," Mrs. Baxter was saying, "it's nothing new with Roger, you know. He's always given us trouble."

"He probably has. But there's a reason—"

"Go on, lady. Take his side of it. Did I hear you say you're a doctor? Just as soon as you give them the money, they take his side of it."

"If I could only make you aware of the damage your son has already suffered. He's in an acute anxiety state and may very well not come out of it."

She heard Mrs. Baxter laugh. "Anxiety state! Honey, that's all I keep hearing. What about what he's been doing to me? I'm human too, you know."

"I'm sure you are," Roberta Clemm said, hating herself for the lie.

"Okay, then, listen—you keep him there until I
get back. Just give me a week. God, I can sure use
some sun. This stinking New York winter—I declare,
I don't know how you people stand it."

"I imagine we're used to it."

"That's it, honey. You are and I'm not. Now
school's out for the Christmas holidays. By the time
they end I'll be back. Then you can just send him
home in a cab. Wait, isn't there a bus there that runs
up to 87th and Riverside Drive?"

Miss Clemm couldn't believe all this was happening. She'd met them all, she thought, but this one—
this one was really something.

"Don't worry," she said. "We'll see that your son
is taken home properly. We'll have to run a few more
tests but he seems to be responding to treatment."

"There, you see?" Mrs. Baxter said. "He always
snaps out of it. You probably worry too much about
it, I guess being a doctor and all."

"Mrs. Baxter, I guess being a doctor and all, as you
put it, may have something to do with it. Don't you
think we ought to have a talk sometime?"

"About what?"

Miss Clemm held the phone away from her face for
a moment. "You know," she said finally, "there's a
word for mothers like you."

And then she told it to her.

CHAPTER TWENTY-TWO

ROBERTA CLEMM parked her car near the corner apartment building and Roger got out.

"Well, so long," he said, starting to walk away. She asked him if he could get into his apartment if his mother hadn't come home yet and he told her a lot of people working in the building had keys. There was a big box of them in the handyman's room, and a whole wall of them on numbered hooks.

"Don't you have your own key?"

"Sometimes," he said, without explaining.

She didn't bother him about it, watching carefully to see that he was all right, wishing she had more time.

"Roger?" she said and he took a step back and leaned closer to her inquiringly. "You have that number I wrote down—"

"Wrote down—not up," he said. "That's funny."

She smiled. "We all say dopey things. Out of habit,

I imagine. But you'll call—if you need me for anything? Please?"

"Don't worry," he said. Then he allowed himself to
grin a little. "Hey, I got 'em pretty good—yes, sir-r-r—
pretty good today. Right? *Right?*"

"You sure did."

"Only I can't depend on it, I guess, huh?"

She spread her hands. "It's like everything else,
sweetheart. You've got to endure—you have to stay
with it and suffer with it and endure—then maybe
it will become a natural part of you. You can't fight
it. You've got to trust it."

"Okay," he said. "Okay. I get the message." He
slapped at his arms and chest. "I feel good now.
Don't worry. I'll keep my mind a blank."

He waved and walked away, and she bit her lip
wishing he hadn't said it quite that way.

Inside, he found nobody in the lobby. One elevator
was working, he saw, its little red button shining. He
jabbed his finger at the black call button, noticing a
wreath hanging next to the elevator wall shaft. *It's
funny*, he thought, *but I keep forgetting it's practically
Christmas.* He wondered idly, looking at the wreath,
why they forgot to put the red holly or a bow on it.

When the elevator car came down there wasn't
anybody in it but George, the moon-faced operator.

"Hi," he said to Roger without much expression.

"Hi," Roger said. Then as the doors started to close,
his hand flicked briefly toward the wreath on the
wall. Trying to be funny and casual, he asked, "Hey,
who died?"

He heard the whine of the mechanism and felt the car start up.

"You been away a week," George said stolidly. "Don't you know? Your girl friend."

"Huh?"

"You know," George's voice was saying, "Miss America upstairs—in the penthouse."

He had to be kidding. Look at him. He's kidding. Isn't he kidding? Well, isn't he? Come on!

"She had a cold and it turned into pneumonia and she died. I guess she didn't have resistance. She went just like *that!*"

George snapped his fingers sharply and Roger wondered, in a strange numb way, why elevator men always wore gloves when the finger-ends had to be cut off anyway.

He didn't remember George stopping the car and locking it in place while he got his key out to open the apartment door, but he must have followed him. There were some white and colored envelopes on the carpet inside the door, and he walked over them as it closed.

Then he was standing alone in the apartment. He was near the cold glass doors leading to the terrace and looking out at the sky but he really didn't see it. There was a funny sound coming from some place. He didn't know he was making it. It was like the sound of humming but made evenly, a single descending note that slurred and then repeated itself.

It was dark in the apartment when She came home. She unlocked the door and put Her bags down.

"Why are you sitting there in the dark?" She asked

and switched on the lamp of the end table. Then She bent down and picked up the mail. "You live here too," She said. "The least you can do is help keep this place clean."

Then She was ripping open the envelopes, exclaiming over the Christmas cards. He didn't hear Her but just kept on with his humming sound.

"Holy cow!" She said shrilly. "What's this?"

The card had wreaths and lighted candles, and red lettering on it. Her eyes were scanning the two rows of green type, one headed *305 Riverside Drive. 86th Street Side*, the other *305 Riverside Drive. 87th Street Side*. There were eighteen names under each heading and opposite each the occupation.

"They all got their hands out," She muttered savagely. "Come Christmas, they all want something. Just look at this, will you?" She waved the card and started to walk across the room to where he was, reading their names, stumbling over some.

"We got a Superintendent," She said sarcastically, "Louis Sontay; and two handymen, Charles Conwick and Joe Abisio; and elevator men Anthony Halsteter, Sam Zumba, and Carlos Brazaga—did you ever in your life hear such names—as well as George Schneider, Angelo Civelli and Carmine Coffi, elevator *relief* men; and Clark Harold, another elevator man; and—" Her eyes refused to scan the names now and jumped to the righthand side "—another elevator relief, a doorman night, a porter, a doorman day, elevator relief, venetian blind man, service car rear, and relief service car!"

"And that's just one side," She raged seeing the

names facing Her on the opposite side of the card. "There's the whole damn 87th Street side too. My God, am I supposed to tip all of them?"

She was near enough to him now to drop the card so that he could catch it but he let it go by. "Here," She said, "if you want a good laugh, read that!"

And then She saw he was just sitting there paying Her no attention. She bent and picked up the card and thrust it at his chest.

"I said, *read* it. You're the one who always thinks money just grows on trees. Now take a look at where it's going!"

When he didn't take the card being shoved at him She became angry. She slapped him and said, "Pay attention when I'm talking."

She cocked her head back and he was still sitting there with the sound coming softly in its cadence from his lips. She switched the light on near him.

"Mother's home," She said. "You know you haven't said a word of greeting? Not a single word. Aren't you interested in if I had a good time?" He still sat there, without paying attention, and She slapped him again, knocking his head back against the couch. "Are you going to talk to me or not? Who the hell are you to freeze me out?"

When he didn't cry or complain or say anything but just continued to sit there, rocking a little now as he made the sound, She became angrier. She hit him several more times.

Then the door opened and Roberta Clemm came in. She stood there for a moment unnoticed and finally when she couldn't stand it another second, she let the door slam behind her. Mrs. Baxter looked up then and stopped what she was doing.

"Who are you and what do you want—and where do you get off busting in here without knocking?"

Miss Clemm pointed to the boy sitting there rocking. "He could tell you who I am—if he could talk." She moved closer to Roger's mother, her grim jaw jutting at an alarming angle. "I'm Dr. Clemm."

She reached out a hand for Roger and Mrs. Baxter shoved it away and told her to get out.

"This is a personal matter," she said. "Strictly between *us*."

"So is this," Miss Clemm said, hitting the surprised woman squarely on the jaw, knocking her into a tumbling twisting heap on the couch. Then she leaned over and extended her hand to Roger. He didn't take it because he wasn't noticing anything. She shook her head and leaned down and picked him up. "He'll be at the hospital," she told Mrs. Baxter, "and I believe you'll be in jail."

Then they went out and she closed the door.

CHAPTER TWENTY-THREE

HE SAT on the edge of his hospital cot for the next two days dangling his feet. He made no other voluntary movement. He didn't look at any part of the room. Not up or sideways, but only at his moving bare feet, his expression neither sad nor bitter, just kind of neutral. Sweet, perhaps, or disinterested. But you had to look for that. He gave you absolutely nothing. Somehow he wasn't really there.

Miss Clemm came at intervals and sat with him and spoke gently but he never looked at her and didn't appear to notice she was speaking.

The nurse came and fed him and he ate a little of what there was, mechanically, unprotestingly. When he had enough, he would make a sound as light as a sigh, and then when she took the plate away he continued staring at his revolving feet.

At the end of the first day he stopped the humming sound that might have been taken for a kind of moaning.

His father came in from Hollywood on the third day but Roger appeared not to notice. His father tried speaking to him or sometimes telling small jokes and laughing but the boy was interested only in his toes.

The father sat patiently for a few hours and then he looked at his watch and told Roger he'd be back soon. He asked the nurse outside where he could get a cup of coffee and then where the phone was. When he got back, he could tell the boy hadn't even noticed his absence.

He had promised Miss Clemm before he first went inside that he wouldn't try to touch the boy and he kept his word, although as he was leaving his hand nearly went to the staring boy's shoulder to pat him.

He spoke with Miss Clemm in the office afterward and asked what it was all about and she explained a little of the schizophrenia withdrawal pattern. She told him, since he seemed interested, something of the mechanism of negativism and how the schizoid reacted this way to a world of reality that was too threatening and frustrating. It was the only way he could shut out these currents before they drowned him, she explained. Harsh perfectionistic mothers and detached fathers helped, too, she said.

The father's eyes were bewildered and a little frightened when she told him his son was in an infantile autistic state at the moment, and that she was hoping he would halt this regressive condition and in time his frozen maladaptive behavior would respond to therapy.

"I don't care how much it costs," the father said when he left. "Money's no object with me here."

"You're still making the same mistake," Miss Clemm told him. "Money never had any meaning for the boy. All that was needed was a little love and understanding. Don't you wave your checkbook to me now after he's made himself disappear."

The father drew back at her vehemence. "Well," he said with a smile he tried to make conciliatory, "do what you can for the kid, huh?"

"Oh, go away," she said, and left him standing, fiddling with his snapbrim hat.

On the fourth day, Roger recognized Miss Clemm's voice and played with the rubber ball she brought him. He bounced it all that day. At night, he sat on the floor with it and rolled it to the wall and watched it bounce gently off and spin back to him.

He smiled at her on the fifth day when she provided some paper and drawing crayons. When she came back later she saw he hadn't drawn anything, but instead had printed a name in large sprawling childish letters:

Roger

Tunnell

The big man stood at her desk stolid in his grief.

"I don't know what it's about, Mr. Tunnell," Miss Clemm said. "But you must be very dear and important to this boy. Yours is the first note of reality he's reached out for. You're our only hope. Would you happen to know why he thought of you?"

"It is quite simple, really," the man said in his deep accented voice. "We both were in love with the same girl." And when she looked up at him, her eyes a little wider with surprise, he added, "She died last week. A day before he came home."

He entered the room quietly and sat in the spare chair, holding his black hat in his hand and wearing his black coat. He didn't speak to the boy sitting on the floor tapping the ball to the floor, then spinning it in circles over and over again.

He sat there motionless, for several hours. Then the ball got away from the boy's fingers and rolled off. The man leaned down and stopped it. The boy came crawling over on his hands and knees, saw the ball was there and reached his hand out for it.

Silently the man gave him the ball.

He sat near the man, near his shining black shoes, spinning the ball. Then he stopped the spinning and looked up at the sad eyes deep in the harshly-etched granite face. The man looked back at him. Neither spoke nor showed any expression. Then Roger's eyes went back to the ball. He held it up.

"*Qu'est-ce que c'est?*" he asked.

"*Une balle,*" the man said. "A ball."

Roger nodded his head. Then he pointed his finger

to himself, tapping his chest. "*Qu-est-ce que c'est?*"

"*Le garcon,*" the big man said. "*C'est le garcon.* It is the boy."

Roger looked up as if puzzled, then shook his head and tapped his chest again.

"*Qu'est-ce que c'est?*" he asked.

"You mean—*comment dit-on en français?*—how Roger."

He shook his head again and tapped once more.

"You mean—*comment di-on en françaisz?*—how does one say it French?"

The boy nodded and he told him, dropping the final R: "*Roger.*"

"*Roger,*" Roger said, imitating the French accent.

He got up, pulling himself up, holding onto the man's knee. Then he reached out and his hand touched Tunnell's hard face. The big man sat quietly and let him touch it.

"*Qu'est-ce que c'est?*"

"My face? It is called *visage*. V*isage*, the face."

"*Visage,*" Roger said.

He put his finger lightly across Tunnell's lips.

"The mouth," Tunnell said. "*La bouche. La bouche,* the mouth."

Then Roger put his finger to something that was glistening at first and then dropping slowly down the rugged furrowed cheek. "*Qu'est-ce que c'est?*" he asked.

"A tear," said the man softly. "*Une larme. Une larme,* a tear."

Then Roger put his hand to his own face and was surprised to find something moist there too. He touched it and saw it wet on the end of his finger.

"*Une larme*," he said.

He came closer and let his head drop to the massive chest of the man sitting there dressed in black. Heavy arms reached out for him and he felt the strength of the Frenchman's fingers as he was pressed close.

Hey! he thought, *I can feel that. I guess I'm back.*

Laurel-Leaf Library Fiction by
KIN PLATT

THE BOY WHO COULD
☐ **MAKE HIMSELF DISAPPEAR** $1.25 (90837-X)
Roger Baxter, new to New York and very lonely, found it hard
to make friends. Gradually, he found it easier to make himself
disappear. "Few novels have the poignancy and shock value
of this touching story."—*The Saturday Review.* A major motion
picture.

☐ **CHLORIS AND THE CREEPS** $1.25 (91415-9)
Eleven-year-old Chloris Carpenter vividly remembers her father,
and when her mother remarries, Chloris wrestles with the
resentment which her stepfather arouses in her. "The author's
handling of real problems is expert and convincing in this
excellent novel."—*Publishers Weekly*

☐ **HEADMAN** $1.25 (93568-7)
A novel born of the streets and written in uncensored street
talk, HEADMAN centers on Owen Kirby, a boy who won't join
any of the more than 300 street gangs in L.A. "As direct as a
hammer blow."—*The New York Times Book Review.* An ALA
Notable Book.

☐ **HEY, DUMMY** $1.25 (93548-2)
When 12-year-old Neil Comstock befriends Alan Harper, a
brain-damaged boy of 13, he must face the cruel taunting of
fellow students and the outrage of his frightened parents. "Sel-
dom is the mentally retarded child so truly and sensitively
portrayed. Highly recommended."—*Best Sellers*

At your local bookstore or use this handy coupon for ordering:

| **Dell** | **DELL BOOKS**
P.O. BOX 1000, PINEBROOK, N.J. 07058 |

Please send me the books I have checked above. I am enclosing $_____
(please add 35¢ per copy to cover postage and handling). Send check or money
order—no cash or C.O.D.'s. Please allow up to 8 weeks for shipment.

Mr/Mrs/Miss_____

Address_____

City_____State/Zip_____